Guns of
Rio
Conchos

Also by Clair Huffaker
in Thorndike Large Print

Badge for a Gunfighter
Cowboy
The Cowboy and the Cossack
Posse From Hell
Seven Ways from Sundown
The War Wagon

GUNS OF RIO CONCHOS

Clair Huffaker

THORNDIKE PRESS • THORNDIKE, MAINE

Library of Congress Cataloging in Publication Data:

Huffaker, Clair.
  Guns of Rio Conchos.

  1. Large type books. I. Title.
  [PS3558.U325G8 1985] 813'.54 84-26820
  ISBN 0-89621-606-3 (lg. print)

Large Print edition available through arrangement with Clair
Huffaker Company.

Cover design by Mimi Harrison

Guns of
Rio
Conchos

APRIL 1874

The First Month

1

There were eight Comanche warriors.

They were quietly sitting their horses, lined up single file, and waiting still as stone on the rim of a far-off hill.

The tall man saw them first. He gave no sign that he had seen them, letting his big pinto continue at a slow, deliberate walk. He said softly to the rough-looking, bearded man riding beside him, "Take it easy, Harry. Just keep moving the way you are."

The bearded man turned a square, sullen face toward the tall man. "What you talkin' about, Riot?"

"We got some friends up ahead, waiting to give us the key to West Texas."

Startled fear jumped into Harry's eyes and the man named Riot spoke sharply. "I said take it easy! Just keep walking your horse."

Harry glanced ahead, then lowered his eyes to the valley floor, a few feet ahead of the horses' hoofs. He said in a high-pitched whisper, "I ain't got your eyes. I didn't see 'em. How many? How far?"

"I make it eight. About half a mile."

"Well, for God's sake, let's turn and make a run for it!"

"No good. They're in plain sight. Expect us to see them sooner or later. That means most likely they got some of the boys spotted behind us by now. Maybe to the sides, too."

"What the hell we goin' to do?"

Riot showed even white teeth in a quick smile that flashed brightly against the deep tan of his strong, fine-featured face. "Well, Harry, if you get any greener, you can just lie down in the grass and they'll never find you."

The bearded man's nervousness was beginning to affect his horse, a scraggly dun, and on top of the too tight rein, the dun now took offense at the faint Indian smell brought to him on the wind, an odor of sweat and old buffalo robes and slightly spoiled meat. The dun's nostrils quivered and its ears went sharply forward.

"Oh, God," Harry moaned, trying to hold the animal to a natural walk, "I should never have left Alpine with you."

Riot stretched his long, powerful arms slowly, as if he were sleepy, and pushed up on the back rim of his expensive, wide-brimmed black hat so that his clear, dark gray eyes were almost hidden, and he had a logical excuse for still not seeing the braves ahead. "There was no invitation. As I recall, they were considering hanging you, too." His gaze swept to the right and left. They were moving north along a wide, shallow valley. To the left, the Davis Mountains broke up the ground. Fort Davis lay that way, and close by, the valley slope to the left was dotted with big boulders that would give some cover.

"I just looked up an' saw 'em," Harry whispered with rising panic. "You know why they didn't wait in hidin' and fill us fulla arrows? 'Cause they wanna play a game!" His voice broke. "They wanna chase us down alive so they can put us t'death slow! I heard about them doin' that!"

Riot nodded briefly. "Yes, it's a game. And we are about to give them some sport. Ready?"

Twisting the stud's body between his legs, Riot hauled him suddenly and hard to the left. He swatted him on the rump, roared, "Wahoo!" at the top of his husky voice and raked the paint with his spurs, all in the same instant.

Driven by pain and fear, the stallion bounded into a dead run on its first leap, its legs a blinding spur of speed as it raced toward and then up the valley slope.

Riot turned his head quickly to the right and the left as his stud struggled up the incline with the dun behind him. His gray eyes took in at a swift glance everything that was to be seen. The eight Comanches to the north were now coming on at a full gallop, riding easily and gracefully, not wasting energy in yells or needless motions. At the lower end of the valley six other Indians dashed into view, and across the valley, directly behind Riot and the other man, two warriors were pushing their horses at full speed down toward the valley floor.

Riot's revolver appeared in his right hand, and he thumbed the hammer back as his paint leaped in great, swift bounds toward the top of the slope.

There were three Comanches waiting beyond the rim of the valley. Riot's pinto burst over the crest of the slope and before its hind hoofs had come down for its first stride on the flat top of the hill, Riot shot one of the braves in the chest. The warriors were closing in, about five galloping paces away. As the first one to go down slid lifelessly from his pony, the others raised rifles and fired together. Riot ducked low

10

over his pinto's neck and raced straight toward them. He heard a slug sing viciously past his head, and the saddle under him was jarred as though someone had hit the pommel with a sledge hammer. He fired a second time, holding his gun so close to the horse's head that the animal swung hard away from the noise, almost tripping himself up. Riot's second shot, aimed at the closest of the two remaining braves, was pulled off just as the Indian's horse reared, throwing its head up. The bullet caught the horse under the jaw and the pony kept on going up and over backwards, screaming with pain. The Indian almost threw himself clear, but one leg was under the crushing backbone of the animal as it slammed down to the ground. It rolled, kicking wildly, and a hind hoof smacked loudly against the side of the Comanche's head.

The third brave fired again as Harry came over the valley top on his dun. Riot's pinto sagged as the point-blank bullet crashed into it. The big man on the dying paint was only one good jump from the last warrior. There was no time for him to thumb back his Colt and fire again. He heaved savagely on the reins with his left hand, almost lifting his horse, now on its last, rearing jump, so that it veered slightly and ran head on into the steeldust Indian pony. As the big paint battered into the smaller steeldust,

Riot brought the Colt barrel around in a long, looping swing that hit the brave across the temple. And then both riders and both horses went down in a thrash of confused movement.

Riot was out of the saddle as the steeldust struggled frantically for footing. At that moment Harry raced by, still spurring his dun to greater speed. Riot was vaguely aware that the dun's light-colored underbelly was red with blood, and then the Comanche who'd been thrown from his steeldust sat up and swung his rifle toward Riot.

Riot pulled the trigger of his Colt and slapped the hammer back with his left hand; it was the quickest way to get off a shot. The Comanche was knocked back onto the ground, his rifle banging before it was on a line with the tall man.

Grabbing the rope bridle hanging from the terrified Indian pony's jaw, Riot kept the plunging animal from running away. He twisted his left hand in the reins and with his right leaned down to take his Winchester from its saddle holster. Going down, the big paint had twisted the saddle slightly under him, and it was impossible to wrench the rifle out of its leather casing. Riot could hear approaching hoofbeats now.

He gave up with the Winchester and cursed.

He glanced briefly at the beautiful worked silver on the black leather saddle. The solid silver top of the pommel was dented where the rifle bullet had hit it a glancing blow. No time for the rifle or saddle now. He grabbed the saddlebags behind the cantle and heaved hard, and the holding thongs snapped. Better than two thousand dollars in the bags. He had that anyway. Now all he had to do was live long enough to spend it.

Riot picked up the Comanche's rifle. He put the saddlebags over the steeldust's withers and leaped aboard, jerking the pony's head around toward where Harry was disappearing in the distance.

The steeldust bounded away from the edge of the valley in long, wiry strides, gaining rapidly on the slower dun. Riot estimated he was something better than three hundred yards from the valley when two parts of the Comanche war party roared up over the edge behind him. The two braves who had been flanking on the far side had joined the half-dozen who had come up from the lower end of the valley. Two groups of eight, separated by maybe a quarter of a mile.

The warrior closest to Riot, a red-shirted brave on a huge buckskin, was still too far for accurate shooting. Still, he raised his rifle and there was the distant crack of a shot.

Immediately following the solitary shot, a thunder of riflefire swept the land behind Riot, and bullets hissed, whined and thudded around him. The racket of repeating rifles in full blaze shattered the air for several seconds, and then settled to sporadic cracks.

When Riot brought the swift steeldust abreast of Harry's dun, he said, "Seems to me they've got some new rifles and we're being used for target practice."

The bearded man cringed even lower on the dun's neck as a slug whistled high over his head. He pulled a Navy revolver from his belt and started shooting back, not bothering to aim, just pointing the gun in the general direction of the Comanches who were closest on the right and behind them. "What'll we do?" he cried.

"Right now we run like hell. And before I forget, thanks for your help back there."

"You didn't have no horse! I thought you was done!" Harry saw that the steeldust was pulling ahead of the dun and he called, "Don't leave me! Your horse's faster'n mine!"

"Some fellows have all the luck." Riot pushed the Indian pony ahead as fast as it would go toward the Davis Mountains, and it edged slowly away from the dun.

"I woulda helped you!" Harry screamed. "I wanted t'help you but I couldn't think how!"

"You're helping me now," Riot called back. "They'll waste some time on you before they get to me."

When the tall man raced his pony into the foothills leading to the mountains, the dun was far behind. A Comanche rifle slug tore into the dun's left hind hoof and ripped it apart. The injured horse tried to continue its run as Harry's spurs raked its shredded flanks, but after a few, lumbering, off-balance strides it went down suddenly on its knees.

Riot turned in time to see Harry start to run on foot. The Comanches did not try to overtake him. They slowed down and began taking pot shots at the running man. Harry went sprawling once, then struggled up and kept going. The second time he went down he stayed down. The Indians formed a circle around him and there were a few more shots.

Reaching the top of a steep foothill where a wagon-sized rock would protect him and the steeldust, Riot slid from the pony's back and leveled the Indian's rifle over the breastwork.

He had noticed that it was a .56 Spenser with a lever action. Now he saw that it was so new there was still a light film of packing oil on the outside of the breach. Sighting carefully, allow-

15

ing for distance, Riot shot into the massed group of Comanches far away and below. Five shots later, one horse was down and two were galloping away without riders as the war party dispersed quickly and started toward him once more. Then the rifle hammer fell on an empty chamber, and Riot left the gun with the barrel extending over the rock. Maybe the sight of the barrel would make them hesitate a little, wondering if he were behind it. Not much chance, but an empty gun was no good to him. He led the steeldust a few feet down the far slope of the foothill, then mounted it and pushed it into a dead run once more.

Reloading his Colt as he held the reins in the crook of his left arm, Riot studied the mountains looming ahead. Judging the steeldust's endurance, he decided it wouldn't have the staying power of, say, the big buckskin he'd seen. There would be others behind him who could outrun his mount in time. Therefore the flats stretching away to his left were no good. Riot knew Fort Davis to be somewhere ahead, but just where, he was not sure. The mountains were new to him. His best bet was to try to keep his lead and get into the roughest part of the hills. Dodge and duck and hold out till night fell. That would be in about three hours – a long time. There were clouds forming in the sky. It would be a dark night.

Ahead of him and to his right, Riot saw a half-mile long, narrow shelf leading to the mountains. On each side of the two-to-three-hundred-foot-wide shelf the ground fell away almost straight down for forty feet. The level top of the shelf was covered with thick, knee-high grass.

He headed for the shelf.

When his now-lathered steeldust brought him to the far end of the long shelf he glanced behind and saw the Comanche war party nearly a third of the way out onto the grassy level. There was a small Mexican piñon pine growing at the edge of the drop-off to his right, and he brought the pony to a stomping halt near it. The wind was just right.

"You're going to have the daylights scared out of you, horse," he said, jumping from the steeldust's back and keeping a tight hold on the reins. He kicked down with a boot at the base of the small piñon and snapped the wrist-thick trunk of the tree. Grabbing it, he pulled hard and ripped the pine free of its base.

Riot crushed the branches together under his boot and, taking a match from his pocket, he flicked his thumbnail over the end of it, then cupped the small flame in his hand and held it to the thick, dry pine needles underfoot.

The needles instantly crackled into flame

and Riot whipped the tree back and forth to work the fire up.

Though they were still out of range, the oncoming Indians began shooting again as Riot sprang back onto the terrified pony. Almost breaking the steeldust's jaw to keep him from bolting away, Riot leaned low off his back and raced him toward the other side of the shelf, dragging the now roaring torch through the tall grass behind him. Fanned by the wind, the grass blazed up instantly as the huge, crackling ball of fire was dragged through it.

At the far side of the shelf Riot swung the steeldust hard to keep the panicked animal from running straight out over the drop before him, and threw the still-blazing pine to the ground. He noticed that his jacket sleeve was smoking with heat, almost ready to go up in flame, and he rubbed the sleeve hard against his leg as the steeldust suddenly screamed with fear and outraged pain. The pony's tail was on fire.

Leaving the ground altogether in a great leap, the wiry horse kicked back savagely in mid-air. His legs scissoring hard into the animal's sides to keep from falling off, Riot twisted around and grabbed the tail near the base and, holding tight, he ran his hard-gripping hand over the length of the lashing tail, crushing out the fire.

Spinning the steeldust into the right direction, Riot gave him his head and the animal barreled up into the mountains and away from the now thundering fire behind.

At a raised outcropping of stones Riot pulled the pony to a brief halt and turned to see what was going on.

The grass fire was sweeping back along the shelf, flames licking high into the air and dense smoke rolling at an angle into the sky. The Comanches were in full-scale rout, rushing back in the only direction they could ride. Spurts of the fiercely burning yellow grass, backed by the wind, darted on ahead of the main line of fire, like searching fingers, and one of these fingers reached out to touch an Indian at the rear of the fleeing Comanche war party. The brave's horse leaped into the air and came down on its side. The rider landed clear of the pony and ran to the edge of the shelf. He lowered himself over the side and climbed down a few feet before the loose rock and clay gave way. He fell more than thirty feet to the ground below.

Riot pulled the steeldust around and galloped on into the mountains, soon losing sight of the Indians, although the smoke from the grass fire could now be seen for miles. He figured there was now better than a mile of broken country between himself and the Comanches. Enough room to breathe.

And then, moving quickly down into a rocky gully, the tired, still frightened steeldust missed its footing. It stepped into a wide crack between two rocks and sank into some soft dirt. Balance gone, it fell to its side as Riot jumped free with the reins still in hand. There was a distinct crack of sound as the animal rolled over once and came to rest on the gully floor, its leg broken.

"Damn," Riot said.

He reached under his black corduroy jacket and pulled a knife from the sheath at his belt and cut the steeldust's throat to put it out of pain. Wiping the blade on some oak grass, he picked up the saddlebags that had fallen from the pony's withers and continued on foot up the gully, returning the knife to its place as he walked.

Beyond the rocky gully there was a sloping incline that led on up higher into the mountains. Riot moved up the incline until he came to a flattened-out plain that was spotted with huge rocks and boulders, and here he began to move very carefully, stepping only from rock to rock and leaving no mark on the earth between. At one point he deliberately crushed some oak grass under his shoe and left a toe mark pointing off to the left. Then he went at a sharp angle to the right.

Maybe the Comanches wouldn't follow him anyway. It had been an expensive day for them. They were behaving foolishly. The party should have split up at the shelf, some taking the lower ground. At this point it was hard to guess what they might do.

They did follow him.

The sun was behind the mountains and there were about two hours of daylight left when Riot heard them coming. He was at the far end of the rock-filled plain when he heard the distant thudding of unshod hoofs on stone. He put the saddlebags over his shoulder and climbed a jagged rock to take a look.

Taking off his hat, he peered over a slab of stone a few yards up from the ground. Far back among the rocks he could see four Comanches wandering, apparently aimlessly, through the natural piles of boulders. During the next few seconds he counted five more. They were split up, searching the rocks to scare him out.

Riot ducked back down and shook his head. They had their work cut out for them. There were a thousand hiding places in that wide, rocky flat. There was one about six feet away from Riot, a rough declivity about twice the size of an iron bathtub. He lay down in it and stared thoughtfully at the darkening blue sky. . . .

21

It was early dark before they came near the tall rock in which he was hiding. Riot inched his head up and saw that they were building a small fire in a clearing an easy stone's throw from where he was crouched. The big brave in the red shirt was speaking in a commanding voice, and as he finished talking four of the Comanches rode away into the night. Riot spoke some Ute, and so could make out roughly what was being said. The big man, Blood Shirt, was war chief of the small party. He'd sent men around the edges of the rocky plateau looking for sign, and, finding none, they'd figured rightly he was still someplace on the plateau. The four men riding out were to patrol the edges and make sure he didn't get away during the night.

Riot caught snatches of their talk which he translated variously as "Thunder in the head," "Jumping eyes," and "Knife that cuts the scalp without touching the hair." After some confusion, he finally decided that the Comanches were all suffering gigantic hangovers. This was verified when one of them said something about a great trade-feast they'd visited the night before.

A short, stocky brave produced a haunch that had been fresh-cut from one of the dead horses and they threw it on the fire briefly before slashing pieces from it to eat. As soon as they'd eaten enough, they lay down on the dirt ringing the fading campfire and went to sleep.

Moving soundlessly from his hiding place, Riot climbed down the jagged rock, the saddlebags still over his shoulder. The Comanche ponies were tethered beyond the camp, and he had to go around the sleeping group. Feeling his way carefully, it took him nearly half an hour to go about thirty yards, and even so the horses became fidgety as he approached them.

He'd thought the ponies were by themselves, but as he stepped closer to them and they moved slightly and snorted almost inaudibly, he saw the outline of a brave's back on one of the mounts. He'd been guarding them, and was now sleeping astride one of them.

Riot was only a few feet behind the warrior on the horse. He rushed forward silently, drawing his knife, and vaulted up behind the Comanche. The horse shrilled with astonished fright and reared up, breaking away from the tether rope, and Riot drove his knife into the back of the brave before shoving him to the ground.

Leaning down, he slashed the rope holding the other animals and let out a blood-chilling yell that echoed against the surrounding hills. The Comanche camp was swarming to life now, and as the scared, bewildered horses scattered, Riot rode with them, riding low along his pony's neck.

At the edge of the plateau he ran almost head on into one of the Indians on patrol. The brave had heard him coming in the dark and was waiting, almost invisible in the deep shadows of a huge rock. Riot saw a flick of movement and felt a savage pain in his chest, although he heard no shot. He raised his revolver and fired twice into the shadows, and heard the sound of a body thudding to the ground. Then he was free and galloping over a smooth, gentle rise. The only trouble was that his head felt hollow, and he was very tired. . . .

Some time later he was dimly aware that he was no longer on the horse. He was lying on the ground in the dark. He sensed trees near his side and crawled into them to be hidden, and to rest.

Either he'd been hit, he told himself with slow thoughtfulness, or . . . he hadn't been getting enough sleep lately.

And then everything was black, and there were no stars or shades of dark within the blackness. . . .

Much later, out of the inky nothingness, he heard with distinct clarity, the voices of men.

"Here he is! Up in the thicket! Jesus' mother,

he's got a arrow square in the chest!"

"He rid near eight mile with that damn thing in 'im!"

"You gotta say one thing for the man. He sure died hard."

"Ain't dead yet."

"No?"

"Nope. Give me a hand here. See if we can get this arrow out of him."

There was silence for a moment, and Riot had the idea that someone, somewhere, was being hurt.

"Ahh! Got it. Way the end was busted, I thought I'd never get a good enough grip."

"You got the arrow okay. But the head come off. Damned thing's still inside 'im."

And then the voices became muddled and distant, and at last dissolved away into nothing.

2

When the blackness around him began to break up, Riot first saw dim, blurred objects of gray and white. He struggled to see better, straining to focus his eyes on the objects. After a long time he made out a ceiling above him and a window to his right where a striped cat was sitting licking its paws. He was in bed, and near the foot of the bed there was a young boy. He was hatless and freckled and he was staring at Riot with intense curiosity. As soon as Riot's eyes rested on him, the boy said, "My name's Tom. I already called Paw, soon as I saw you was comin' around."

Riot blinked. He planned to answer the boy, but when he reached for his voice, it wasn't there.

"Paw's in the barn. Mister, do you know how long you been in that bed?"

Evidently Riot managed to shake his head slightly, for the boy said, "I'll tell you how long. Nearly two weeks! Some of the time you'd sit up and talk like crazy, and you were fevered somethin' awful. Doc White said it's a miracle you ain't dead. I'm glad you're coming out of it. There's a million questions I been wantin' to put to you."

There was a sound behind the boy, and the door opened. A square-built man with an iron-gray beard walked into the room, followed by a tall man about Riot's age, the middle twenties. The older man stared at him for a long moment, his keen, piercing eyes bold beneath heavy eyebrows. "How do you feel?"

Finding at least part of his voice, Riot murmured, "Horrible."

There was a quick glint of humor in the older man's eyes. "You were on the fence there for a while. I'm Ben McCallister. My son, Thaddeus. And that midget leering at you from the foot of the bed is Tom."

Riot swallowed and said, "Riot."

Ben McCallister frowned, not quite understanding, and then said, "Riot it is."

"Riot Holiday." He shoved up with his elbows, finding strength there, and got into a half-sitting position. "How did you find me?"

Thaddeus spoke for the first time. He was an

27

honest, tough-looking young man with blue eyes and a big, straight-lined mouth. His words came out firm and were well thought out. "The trail was clear-marked — with dead Comanches."

"What place is this?"

McCallister moved his hand a few inches, thinking of and taking in the wide, flat square miles of land beyond the confines of the house. "My ranch. The Double M."

A small, thin woman with a bird's quick eye and gentle lines around her mouth came into the room. "You've talked with him enough, Ben. He'll want his rest."

"Yes, Martha."

They all left the room and a moment later the woman reappeared with a bowl of broth. She spoon-fed Riot silently, frowning away his weak attempt to sit up and feed himself. When she'd finished she said, "The doctor will be here tomorrow, God willing."

Riot thought he saw a faint look of troubled concern pass through her eyes. "I don't need a doctor," he said. "I'm right side up."

She nodded briefly, and though she didn't smile she made her lips crinkle at the edges. "Yes, you are." She stood up. "Get some more rest now."

Closing his eyes, Riot drifted out into space,

and when he came back to the solid world once more there was an elderly tight-faced soldier standing beside the bed. "Mr. Holiday. I'm Dr. Gates, Army surgeon from Fort Davis."

Mildly surprised at his own clarity of mind, Riot said, "What happened to Dr. White?"

"He's been and gone. Thaddeus McCallister rode to the fort to bring me over here. Mr. Holiday, you're in trouble. No point beating around the bush."

"Trouble?"

Gates nodded. "You've got a steel arrowhead lodged next to your aorta — the large trunk artery directly above your heart. As I say, the arrowhead is steel, and it comes to a fairly sharp point. At least we can assume that. The arrow entered your chest, glancing slightly off one rib and entering deeply. Right now it's located, as I say, next to the aorta, and directly above the right ventricle." He hesitated and rubbed his jaw, avoiding Riot's eyes. "Reason I'm explaining all this is because . . . an operation to remove that arrowhead would be impossible."

"So?"

"Mr. Holiday, both Dr. White and I are veterans of the Civil War. We've each seen cases to one degree or another similar to yours. We are in agreement. Any attempt to remove the piece of steel would be fatal to you. You should be

29

dead right now, by all rights. Moreover, that steel will not remain where it is. It will move within you. And since it seems to be pointing toward the aorta, it will eventually pierce that vessel. Muscular exertion could cause it to move; so could a sharp blow above the arrowhead. The amount of time you have left is partly up to you. Dr. White and I agree — as a rough estimate — that if you don't strain yourself too much, you should with luck, live about six months."

Riot said nothing and Gates waited a moment before speaking again. "You understand what I've told you?"

"Yes. It doesn't fit in with my plans at all."

Rubbing a hand through thinning, silver-gray hair, Gates said, "In due time you'll be able to get around a little. Maybe even do some light chores occasionally." He picked up his hat and a small leather bag. "You can get out of bed in about three weeks." At the door, the Army surgeon hesitated. He said, "I'm sorry. And good luck." And then he went out, shutting the door softly behind him.

Before, Riot had planned on going peacefully back to sleep. Now, after hearing what Gates had to say, he braced himself and pushed the blankets away from his chest. There was a tight, foot-wide bandage wrapped around him. Gritting his teeth, Riot called on his legs to move, and they inched up slowly. When he shifted into a sitting position with his legs over the edge of the bed, it felt as if his head was about to fly into the far corner all by itself, but after resting a few seconds he was able to stand up.

His clothes were clean and freshly ironed, stacked on a homemade chest at the wall by the window. It took time and patience and he almost went down twice, but he managed to dress himself and, despite the fiery complaint across his chest, pull his boots on.

Opening the door, he stepped out into the ranch-house kitchen. A girl with long auburn hair was working at the stove, and at the sound of the door closing behind him, she turned around in wide-eyed surprise. Riot took her for eighteen, maybe nineteen. Pretty, with full lips and a sparkle of green in her blue eyes.

"Oh, you shouldn't be up," she whispered.

Riot smiled. "Thought I'd go out for some air."

She wiped her hands quickly on the apron around her slender waist. "I'll help you to the porch."

Not wanting help, Riot hesitated. Then he said, "All right. That's kind of you."

She took his elbow, supporting it with both hands, and walked out with him onto the

31

wooden porch beyond the kitchen. Only when he was safely seated in one of the two rocking chairs there did she release his elbow. "My name is Roslyn, Mr. Holiday."

"Mine's Riot."

The older woman came around the corner of the house carrying an armful of dried clothes and she stopped as she stepped up onto the porch. "You shouldn't be up for three weeks yet," she said with maternal indignation and concern in her voice.

"He wanted some air, Mother," the girl explained. "I'll go tell P — Father, he's up."

As Roslyn left the porch, Mrs. McCallister carried her laundry closer to Riot. "Mother and Father it is now, instead of Ma and Pa. You may have helped Roslyn become conscious of her manners."

"I must have been a load for you to carry, Mrs. McCallister."

She smiled a rare, fleeting smile. "No."

Then, as voices were heard in the barn where Roslyn had disappeared, she headed for the kitchen door. "You men will want to talk."

Ben McCallister came out of the barn, leaned a pitchfork against the door, and headed across the hard-packed dirt for the porch. Behind him in a line came a big young man, Roslyn and the boy, Tom. In the shade of the porch, he said,

"You've not met this good-sized fellow yet, Riot. He's my eldest, Josh."

Josh stepped over to shake hands. He nodded at Riot, but he said nothing. He had his father's steady eye.

Roslyn went on into the kitchen and McCallister sat in the second rocker. "You're up and kicking three weeks ahead of schedule."

"So they tell me."

"Willya tell about the fight, Mr. Holiday?" Tom asked, curiosity bursting out of him. "How many Comanches was there? Didya see Blood Shirt?"

"That's enough," McCallister told the boy. "This talk is for men. Shut up or beat it."

Tom frowned and crossed his arms before him in silence, and his father said, "Now I'll ask the same questions. Do you know how big the group was, and was one of the Comanches wearing a red shirt?"

"There were twenty-one braves that I saw. One of them was Blood Shirt."

"How were they armed?"

"Better than the U.S. Army, which is still plugging along with Springfield single-shots."

Riot saw a speck of movement far out on the flatlands beyond the porch. It was a single rider, and his eyes followed the approaching man and horse as he continued. "Spenser repeaters. At least the one I had hold of for a while was. A brand-new Fifty-six. Hadn't been fired more than a few times." He grinned. "All those rifles, and somehow I got hit with an arrow . . . funny."

McCallister now saw the oncoming rider. "That'll be Thaddeus. He rode to Pecos Bend."

"Thirty miles," Tom said proudly. "To get some special stuff from a apoth'cary there t'make your chest heal."

"Tom," his father said, "go out to the barn and start pitching hay down for the horses." When the boy was gone, McCallister stared thoughtfully at the porch floor. "What you ran into, Riot, was just the start of it. All hell's going to bust out in this land."

"What do you mean?"

"Blood Shirt bought the first few rifles the day before he met you. Some fellows robbed an Army ammunition train back East. Got off with nearly a thousand rifles, and the dear Lord only knows how much ammunition. They got the stuff down to Mexico and made a deal to sell them to the Comanches. The next deal will be the big one. It'll take some time to swing it, probably not till late summer or early fall. But when it happens, there'll be enough modern-armed Comanches to damned near take over Texas."

"How do you know all this?"

"Took a Comanche alive a while back."

"And he told you all that?"

"Yes. He told me." McCallister said no more on the subject of the Indian he had taken.

"I've been wondering about my saddlebags," Riot said.

"They are inside, unopened. I was going to open them if . . . you went off the wrong side of the fence. To see if there might be anyone to write to."

"I've no family."

"No?" McCallister paused. "It's possibly not what you want to do — your clothes don't mark you as a working man — but you are welcome to stay with us on this ranch for as long as you want to."

Riot sensed the older man's discomfort, and he said, "The doctor told you about how long I have left to live?"

McCallister nodded.

Josh spoke for the first time, from where he stood leaning against a porch beam. "We would be pleased to have you stay here."

Riot nodded at a large wagon tongue leaning against one end of the porch. "I'll stay until I can lift that over my head."

McCallister said to Riot, "Son, that's a big ox tongue and it's solid oak. Weighs better than

35

two hundred pounds. Both doctors said you could do only light chores at best."

"I'm not going to die yet. I've got six more months and I'm going to live during the time I got left."

Thaddeus was still far out on the flats when Mrs. McCallister came from the kitchen to the porch. "I'd take it as a favor if you'd lie down for an hour or so, Mr. Holiday. And if you're up to it, you could join us for supper."

McCallister stood up when Riot did, and Riot started to walk by him into the house, then hesitated. "By the way, I've got money in those bags. I'll want to pay you for your trouble, keeping me on here."

The older man's eyes hardened, and Riot realized he hadn't known how tough McCallister could be if he wanted to. "That's the first thing you've said that I didn't like," he told Riot. "Don't make me mad by mentioning it again."

"I'm sorry. But I've always paid my way, with people I've liked."

McCallister's gaze rested searchingly on Riot. "Do me this, then. Don't consider us people you like. Consider us your family."

Uncomfortable, Riot said, "If you knew the kind of man I am, you wouldn't say that."

"Pa's been making quick judgments for fifty years," Josh said. "I've yet to see him mistaken."

"You said my clothes weren't a working man's. You're right there. They're the clothes of a gunman and gambler. Soon as I'm strong enough, I'm going out into the world and do my level best to crowd all the hell-raisin' and fun of a lifetime into the days that are left." Riot stopped talking for a moment, his head getting dizzy. Then he said, "I appreciate your offer. But I got a lot of fighting and drinking and gambling and general roarin' around to do."

The porch floor tipped up toward him, and Josh caught him as he fell. "Easy," McCallister's big son murmured. "You'll have to whisper some before you're fit to roar."

At suppertime it was Thaddeus who touched Riot lightly on the shoulder to awaken him. Riot opened his eyes and the other man said softly, "Ma says a solid meal will be good for you, if you're not too tired. You been living on soup, and you lost a lot of blood."

"Sounds good." Riot got up and gritted his teeth as he pulled on his boots.

Motioning to a small box on the chest by the window, Thaddeus said, "There's some stuff there that's supposed to help you. Pills. You swallow them."

"Heard you rode thirty miles for that little box. I'm obliged."

Thaddeus twisted the hat brim slowly, staring at it as he spoke. "I'm the one who pulled the arrow out of you. Maybe, had I pulled it easier, not been so damned nervous, it would've come out right. I can't help think'in that."

"If you men hadn't come along, I'd still be out there," said Riot. "That's the thing to think on."

Thaddeus breathed deep. "Supper'll be waiting."

Young Tom ate in controlled silence, but when he'd finished he said, "Mr. Holiday, how'd you come by the name of Riot?"

Riot grinned at the boy. "There was a riot in town the night I was born."

"Where was that?"

"Don't pester him," McCallister said. He glanced at Riot. "Up to nine or ten, they're about ten pounds boy and ninety pounds questions."

Riot drank some of his coffee. "Little town called Tooele, in Utah."

After they'd finished coffee, McCallister said, "Get wood for the morning fire, Tom. Then go to bed, huh? You feel up to a cigar, Riot?"

"Sounds great."

"Let's smoke on the porch."

The family got up from table, and for a short time Tom, Roslyn and Riot were alone in the kitchen. Tom chose this moment to say, "Sleep! Boy, you got no idea how lucky you are not to have to sleep with Roslyn."

The girl blushed wildly and got up to hide her distress by quickly starting to clear the table.

"She squirms," Tom said, going out the door toward the woodpile.

Roslyn was getting control of the blush as Riot got slowly up out of the chair. She stopped by the table in her work and said, "You don't ask questions of people, do you?"

"I don't know. I guess not many."

"You never asked how come Father and the three boys happened to find you."

"Three boys?" Riot asked. "Tom was out there with them?"

"No. Ed was. Ed was twin brother to Thaddeus."

"Was?"

She nodded, and her eyes went down. "Pa made out the smoke of the brush fire you set. He took my brothers and the rest of us over to the settlement at Singing Bird Creek. Then he and my brothers and about fifteen men from the settlement went out to see what had made the fire." She glanced up. "The thing I wanted you to know, a thing they'd never tell you, was that the McCallisters were the only ones who

39

had the nerve to go on, after they got an idea how big the war party was. It was Pa and the three boys who went on, alone, and brought you back. I'm proud of them for that, and I wanted you to know they did it."

Riot leaned his hands on the table. "Ed?"

"They were riding back with you when a Comanche took a long shot at them from a rock in the hills. Ed was killed."

Choosing his words, Riot said, "They'd have let me get better and ride out of here, and they'd never have said a word about that. Even little Tom."

"Father told him not to. Afraid for your feelings. I'm going against his wish, telling you. But there's a hardness about you, and I think you'll be a better man for knowing."

The girl abruptly stopped talking and went back to clearing the dishes. Her mother came into the kitchen then, and Riot went out onto the porch.

When the three grown McCallister men and he were well into their cigars, Thaddeus said, "Ran into Joe Norton outside of Pecos Bend yesterday. He said Blood Shirt's been seen up north, pretty high up along the Staked Plains."

"Showing off his new guns to his friends, most like," McCallister said. "He'll be getting to be a big chief, now. Him and his red flannel shirt. He claims it was soaked red in the blood of his enemies. He'd make a top politician back in Washington."

The men spoke in low voices that did not carry, and Riot noticed that out of habit they held their cigars so the glowing tips were almost invisible, cupped in the palms of their hands.

"Norton said three settler families was wiped out in five days not far from the end of the Colorado," Thaddeus went on. "And the last he heard, Blood Shirt was moving south again. Braves are signin' up with him all along the line, and whole tribes are promising to swing over to him once he gets those guns. He's just about got them convinced he's a livin' god."

Josh said, "He din't do so good as a god when he was chasin' after Riot here."

Letting smoke out of his lungs, Riot said, "Isn't somebody doing something about headin' off those rifles?"

"Sure," McCallister said. "Army and the Texas Rangers are doing what they can. Understand they got double patrols along the Rio Grande. But they can't legally go down into Mexico where the guns are supposed to be hidden."

"I'm told," said Riot, "that the one thing a Comanche'd rather shoot than a Texan is a Mexican. Mexican government doing anything?"

McCallister shrugged. "Who knows what the Mexicans are doing, ever?"

There was a long stretch of thoughtful quiet, and then Riot said, "Why do you people do it? Why do you come out to this wild country with your families, and try to make a home?"

There was an edge in his voice that McCallister noted, and the older man looked at him keenly in the shadows of the porch. "You know about Ed."

"Yes."

Ben McCallister sighed and shook his head. "Well, after twelve years out here, Riot, I still can't answer your question about why we do it. Maybe we're crazy." He got up and started for the kitchen door. "Lots to do tomorrow. Going to turn in."

The other three stood up and Josh said, "Pa was hard hit by Ed's passin'."

Thaddeus stepped off the porch and ground his cigar butt out under his heel. "Since the Comanches are gettin' bolder these days, I'm going to sleep in the barn. Spell you off week for week till trail season, Josh."

"Fair enough."

"You afraid they'll run off your stock?" Riot asked.

"We got a built-in burglar alarm against Indians in the barn," Thaddeus told him. "Old

Blue — she's a cow — can smell a savage from half a mile upwind and twenty miles down. And she starts kickin' her stall when she does."

For the better part of two weeks, Riot took it easy on the McCallister's Double M ranch. Against the entire family's protests, he managed to do some work around the ranch. He helped the grown men extend and partition the barn in preparation for some blooded stock McCallister was having delivered from nearby Austin, and he built a tall stool for Mrs. McCallister to sit on while working at the kitchen counter.

On the fifth day, it was Roslyn's nineteenth birthday, and that was the day Riot found out it was her room he was using. He moved his few things into the bunk room with Josh and Thaddeus, and when Roslyn went to her room that night, she found he'd left a bouquet of blue lupines and a fifty-dollar greenback on her pillow as a birthday present. He was kidded the next night by Thaddeus and Josh, when he found a single marigold on his bunk.

Twice in the next two weeks, Riot went out to the big wagon tongue when he thought no one was looking. The first time, all he had to do was look at it to know he couldn't hoist it. The second time, he pulled it away from where it was leaning and raised it a little, but the weight caught at his chest and tightened his muscles uncomfortably. Later that day Thaddeus grinned at him. "Way you're put together, Josh and me both figure you could normally use that ox tongue for a walkin' stick." He turned serious. "Hope you don't keel over the day you pick it up."

"I'd rather die trying to pick it up than waste a lot of time being scared of trying."

Thinking his own thoughts, Thaddeus unconsciously shifted his worn revolver holster so that it rested on his hip in the same position that Riot wore his. He said, "Yeah. I guess you get a feelin' for the importance of time."

That was the night time ran out at the Mc-Callister ranch. And Old Blue gave no warning.

3

A full moon in the dark sky above was sending a glow of silver into the ranch-house bunk room when Riot woke up. Not quite knowing why, he was tense as tight-strung wire, and he sat up and put his legs over the edge of his bottom bunk. Crickets were singing, and yet it was too quiet. Maybe it had been too long since he'd heard the cry of a night bird. He grunted noiselessly. Maybe he'd eaten too much of Martha McCallister's supper. He reached for his boots.

"It got you, too?" Josh spoke softly, slightly raising his big body on the bunk opposite.

"Yeah."

"What is it?"

"Don't know."

Josh crossed to the window and looked out, standing a little to the side of the glass. "Looks peaceful out around the barn."

His boots now on, Riot stood up quietly. "I'll go take a look."

"I'll go."

Riot strapped his gun on. "I'm all set. Come and bar the door behind me. I'll go check Thaddeus, take a walk around."

Barring the window with its tight-fitting, heavy oak shutters, Josh moved out with Riot into the kitchen. Mrs. McCallister came into the kitchen and said through the shadows, "I thought I heard you moving around. I'll light a candle."

"No, Ma. Don't strike a match just yet," Josh said. "Pa awake?"

"No."

"While I let Riot out, will you go back in and close the shutters? I'll get the ones in Tom and Roslyn's room."

She went back through the door without a word, and Riot stepped silently out onto the porch. The shadow cast by the house extended almost to the barn. Crouching down, Riot walked softly, keeping to the shadow until the last few steps, and then he was in the dark building beyond.

He whispered, "Thaddeus?"

In a moment, another whisper came back. "That you, Riot?"

"Yeah."

"What's the matter?"

Riot moved toward the other man, his eyes growing accustomed to the dark. "How's Old Blue?"

"Quiet as a mouse. Anything wrong?"

"Don't know. Josh and me both woke up."

"An Indian's never come near here but what this cow's made a stomp and fuss about it. She even moos sometimes."

"Just the same, I'll feel better if I go out and make a wide circle around the place."

It was then that they heard many softly running footsteps, and a gun blasted the dark air from the direction of the house.

In his stockinged feet, Thaddeus ran to the barn's back door and slammed it shut, throwing down the three-by-four crossbeam that locked it. Riot sprinted to the front door of the barn in time to see shadowy figures swarming around the house, on foot.

Two guns went off at the same time inside the house, and one Comanche yelped in the moonlight as an arm fell limply at his side. The Indians tried to break through the window shutters, slamming stone-headed warclubs and sharp metal tomahawks against them, but the oak held firm. Then Riot and Thaddeus began shooting from the barn and a Comanche called out an order in a high, whooping voice. Within a few seconds the warriors had raced out of sight away from the house, leaving one dead brave sprawled on the ground outside Roslyn's window, and another jackknifed over the porch railing.

From farther out on the flats, pinpoints of fire began to spurt sharply in the night as the Comanches opened up with their rifles. There was a tinkle of glass shattering in the house, and one of the rocking chairs on the porch was knocked over on its side. Riot pulled Thaddeus down as bullets started pounding through the walls of the barn. In a stall behind them a horse grunted in pain as a slug came through the planking and tore into him.

"Think we can make it to the house?" Thaddeus asked calmly.

Riot shooked his head, "Not now."

"God, listen to that noise! All them rifles — it's Blood Shirt for sure."

"Bullets are splitting those shutters to pieces. They'll soon be rushing us again." Riot blinked as a slug smacked the ground in front of him, sending dirt flying in his face. "They ought to be trying to burn the house, and they're not. You figure why?"

"Maybe they're scared somebody'll see the glowin' of the fire in the sky. Settlement's only sixteen miles. There's soldiers there lots of the time."

From behind them there was the squealing sound of pressure-tortured wood on wood, and then a loud crash. "Stay here!" Riot said. He ran back through the dark barn to the far door that was now broken open and hanging on twisted hinges. Two Indian ponies had been backed to the door, then frightened until they broke it with their rumps. One of them was plunging and kicking now, and his hind hoofs were smashing the awkwardly dangling door. A Comanche sprang toward the doorframe. Riot's gun went off and the warrior disappeared. Unhanded, the ponies raced away into the dark, one of them running clumsily, dragging a broken hind leg.

"Thaddeus!" Riot yelled. "They'll be in here soon!" He winced as a slug whined off a beam by his head. "Let's fire the barn!"

"There's kerosene here!" Thaddeus hurried to where a can and two large bottles of the liquid were kept in the barn. He was opening the can to pour the kerosene out when Riot reached the spot. Riot picked up one large bottle, judged position and let fly with it so that it struck the wall above a stack of hay. The bottle smashed against the wood, covering the hay with a shower of glass and kerosene. He sent the second bottle sailing after the first as Thaddeus spilled the rest of it over a pile of wood.

"Throw open the stall doors. Grab a horse's neck and hang on!" Riot took a quick shot at another Comanche, who appeared outside the doorway, then helped Thaddeus let the animals loose.

"What about tryin' for the house?" Thaddeus called.

"We'd do best getting out beyond and deviling them from behind! We'd never make the porch!"

The frightened beasts were milling between stalls now, and Riot scratched a match along the wall, heaving it at the haystack and it spluttered into flame. There was a soft *whump* of exploding oil, and fire raced through the wood and hay. A big gray mare started past Riot on her way to the door away from the fire and he leaped for her neck as she went by, hooking his left foot over her back.

The Comanches started a rush for the door as the terrified animals, nine horses and three milk cows, charged out into them, bowling them to the side as they plunged madly for freedom.

In a burst of speed encouraged by a rifle bullet creasing her rump, the mare sped away from the barn. Out in the dark of the flats Riot dropped from the galloping mare and went rolling as one foot struck a well-rooted branch of sagebrush.

The other animals were scattering in every direction, and when he got up onto one knee, Riot couldn't see or hear any sign of Thaddeus.

Flames were already shooting up through the hayloft and going fifty feet above the barn, lighting up the land around with weirdly dancing shadows. Riot expected riders to come after the fleeing animals, to hunt down the men who had been in the barn. But no one was yet coming after him.

And then Riot knew why. The Comanches were rushing the house and there was little or no firepower from within to stop them. Each of the warriors wanted to be among the first to enter the house, to make a big coup by touching a living enemy, or to collect a scalp.

Riot ducked into a shallow natural ditch that led obliquely toward the house. He ran along it, crouched over, and heard the rhythmic thumping of a battering-ram hitting the door. He tripped over an Indian lying in the ditch and whirled as he fell, his cocked revolver whipping into a line with the prone warrior's body, but the savage was dead. When he got to the point where the ditch was closest to the house, Riot stretched out, head and arms over the bank, and started firing.

There were about eight Comanches on the McCallister porch. They'd taken the big wagon tongue and were swinging it between them to smash in the door. There were still some Indians shooting from the flame-shadowed flats, and others were sprinting toward the porch. Riot got off two quick shots and then ran back along the ditch as he reloaded. There was a moment of confusion among the Indians holding the battering-ram when the one nearest the door slowly let go of the wagon tongue, sat down with his back to the wall and died.

By the time another warrior had jumped up to fill his place, Riot was ready to go again. The porch was getting crowded with eager, yelling braves, anxious to get inside and Riot put six more shots into the close-packed mob in a few seconds.

Howling with pain and fury, the Comanches swarmed off the porch, dropping the wagon tongue and crashing into each other as they fought to get out of the vicious fire from the flats.

Then Riot saw Blood Shirt for the first time. The chief was running from the direction of the flaming barn and he shrieked an order, waving his hand in Riot's general direction. Six or eight braves broke away from the pack and ran swiftly, bent almost double, out toward the flatlands where Riot was loading again.

The running Comanches got to the ditch with its deeper shadows as Riot finished reloading. He ducked down in the dark of the ditch bank, and waited. One of them shouted a few words that Riot took to mean that the others were to go on while he searched the small gully.

As the other braves searched on beyond the ditch, Riot crawled a few feet to the dead Comanche he'd tripped over before. There was a splintering crash from the house and Riot knew the main body of Indians was now pouring into the McCallister kitchen. There was a lot of whooping and yelling but no shooting, and a shot would mark his position. The dead warrior sounded as if he were exhaling breath as Riot pushed him partially around to search his belt. He found a tomahawk and took it out and kept crawling. As the Comanche searching the ditch came closer, Riot waited a few feet beyond the corpse.

The advancing brave's moccasined foot touched the dead man and he hesitated, leaning quickly down to try to see who it was. He sensed a faint movement beyond, and raised his yellow-painted face an instant before Riot hit him in the forehead with the deadly hatchet.

The warrior died soundlessly.

As he pulled the hatchet out of the brave's head, Riot heard a faint volley of shots from far out on the flats. Some of the Comanches heard them too, for a few seconds later a few riders driving a swarm of ponies rode thunderously in from the dark prairie, bringing the horses to a milling halt before the house.

There was a second, louder volley, and the men still searching for Riot ran back into the light cast by the burning barn. Other Comanches were racing from the house with whatever loot they could carry. Riot noticed one of them waving the stool that he'd made for Mrs. McCallister over his head. The Comanches hurried to their horses as Riot heard the faint, flat tones of a bugle, and then the savages were riding swiftly away from the light of the burning barn and into the far darkness beyond.

Riot stood up slowly. He hated to do it, but he had to go into the McCallister House.

4

Holding his gun ready, Riot moved toward the silent, broken house. Above the furious crackling of flames, there was a sudden, rushing roar, and he whirled at the sound. It was the barn roof falling in, and it sent a huge cloud of sparks sailing high into the sky.

Stepping over the bodies in front of the shattered door, he went slowly into the dark kitchen. There was sweat on his hands as he took out a match and struck it on the wall beside him.

Josh lay at his feet. Riot recognized him by the size of his body. There was no other way.

Ben McCallister was half in and half out of his bedroom at the far side of the kitchen. Riot crossed the room, dropping the burned-out match from nerveless fingers, and struck another. Martha McCallister's body was lying across the torn-up bed, her right hand stretched out toward the smaller body that had been Tom, as if to protect the boy even in death. Blood was still flowing sluggishly from the bare flesh where her hair had been.

Riot pushed the door to Roslyn's room, but it was locked. "Roslyn?" he called once. There was no answer, and he raised his right boot and kicked the door down. He struck a third match and held it inside the doorframe. The girl was standing in the far corner of the room, her eyes glazed, a cocked revolver held before her with both hands. The barrel of the revolver was pointed at her own chest.

Riot held the match close to his own face and said very softly, "It's all right, Roslyn. It's me, Riot. The Comanches have gone away. Help is coming." Instinctively, he kept up the gentle talk as he went slowly to the lamp in her room and lighted it. "You see? It's me, Roslyn."

The lamplight flooded into the kitchen through the door Riot had knocked down. Roslyn's eyes moved dumbly beyond the walls of her room into the kitchen. Then she blinked and whispered, "That's Josh! Oh my God, Josh!"

She lowered the revolver and Riot stepped quickly to her and took it, releasing the hammer under his thumb. She started for the kitchen and Riot took her by the shoulders. "Don't go out. There's nothing you can do now. Sit down."

From outside there came the sound of fast-moving horses that Riot knew to be cavalry from the hundred small sounds of metal on metal. "Anyone in there?" a voice called out.

A moment later there were heavy boots on the porch and a lieutenant, revolver in hand, came into the house cautiously with two soldiers behind him. At Roslyn's door the officer stared at them for a long time, as though he didn't really believe they were there.

"I wasn't expecting to find survivors," he said at last. "Why didn't you answer me?"

Riot gently pushed Roslyn away from the wall and, with his hand on her shoulder forced her to sit down on the edge of her bed. He went to the lieutenant and said, "I'd like the girl to be spared seeing this."

One of the soldiers had found an unbroken lamp in the kitchen and he now lighted it. The lieutenant glanced around him, and his heavily tanned face tightened. "Of course." He silently counted four dead Comanches in the kitchen and said, "You put up quite a resistance."

"Not me. Those two were in here alone."

Other soldiers came in through the door and one of them said, "Sir, the scout says it's no good going after them till morning. Sky's clouding up. Too dark to trail."

"Break out a burial detail. And send some men out a ways to dig one big hole for these dead savages."

"I've been lookin' around outside an' in, sir. That'll have to be a damned big hole."

Riot said, "Could you spare a couple of men to take this girl to the settlement? The McCallisters have friends there who'll look out for her."

Later, when Riot helped the girl onto a government-branded pony, she had still said nothing beyond her first words about her brother, nor had she cried. Now she clutched his hand with fierce strength and said, "All of them. All of them gone."

Not believing it himself, Riot said, "Maybe Thaddeus is alive. I'm going to look for him."

"I shouldn't leave my parents alone to be buried. Mother would want to be in her white dress. And she'd want Tom in his blue suit that she bought in San Antonio two years ago." Her voice broke and she whispered, "A prayer should be said over them."

"Miss McCallister," the lieutenant said, moving out of the shadows toward the horse Roslyn was sitting, "please know that we'll do the very best we are able. We will treat them as our own.

But the only safe place for you for several days is the settlement."

"I'll come to see you there," Riot said. He waited until the girl had ridden out of sight with the soldiers escorting her. Then he walked out past the still slowly burning barn, glancing at it as he went by, hoping Thaddeus's body was not under those black embers. A cavalryman riding guard on the dark flats stopped him. "Where you goin'?"

"Out there."

"What for?"

"None of your damned business."

"Lieutenant wouldn't like you walkin' off by yourself."

"Then shoot me." Riot kept going.

The soldier rode along with him a short distance. "Good thing they set the barn to fire. We was on our way into the settlement when we see 'er go up. Not more'n four, five miles off." He reined up, and as Riot continued he called, "Wouldn't go too far out there, mister. That's the way the Indians went."

Riot found Old Blue on a distant rise in the flats. The cow was dead, her hindquarters chopped off to provide fresh meat for the Comanches. After a long, slow search in the dark for Thaddeus, he gave up and started back. He was within hearing of the soldiers at the ranch house, moving toward them from a slightly different direction, when he found Thaddeus stretched out alongside a big, thick ball of sagebrush.

Kneeling on the ground, Riot ran his fingers over the dark figure of the man. There was some caked blood on Thaddeus's forehead, but he was breathing and seemed to be all right. As Riot picked him up, Thaddeus began to move, and still half-unconscious he muttered, "I'm okay. Put me down. We'll go back and hit 'em from the rear!" He wobbled briefly on his own feet, then caught his balance and stared at the barn. "What happened to the barn?"

Riot said, "It's all over. They got into the house. Now they're gone."

"You're crazy, Riot!" It was a hoarse whisper. Thaddeus started to run toward the house and barn. "I see 'em movin' around!"

"You see soldiers!" Riot caught him and grabbed him by the arm, "Put that gun away! The fight's over!" He added in a low voice, putting it the best way he knew how, "Roslyn's still alive."

"Roslyn?" Thaddeus groped for his holster and dropped the revolver in it. "What do you mean Roslyn's still alive?"

"I mean – she came through all right. The others didn't."

Thaddeus sat down on the ground. "Ma and Pa – Josh, Tom. Dead?"

"Yes."

After some time, Thaddeus said, "How long's it been since I come off that horse and banged m'head?"

"I don't know. Quite a while."

"My God. Oh, my God. The first time Old Blue never gave warnin'. She never so much as moved an ear!"

Riot helped Thaddeus to his feet, and they started back toward the ranch house. "Old Blue paid for it," Riot said soberly. "She'll never make a mistake again."

It was not far from the morning's first light when Riot and Thaddeus walked past the place where the barn had stood. They moved silently through groups of soldiers in the yard, and mounted the porch. The lieutenant came out of the door. Seeing Thaddeus, he said, "Another one? You were lucky." He turned his head toward the inside of the house. "They're as ready as can be for burying. We've got some coffins put together."

Thaddeus went into the house alone, and Riot noticed absently that no one had yet bothered moving the wagon tongue from the porch. He picked it up and carried it back to where it had leaned before. Only then did he remember what lifting the tongue meant.

He had done the thing that was to mark the beginning of his last few hell-raising months.

The Second Month

5

The settlement at Singing Bird Creek was a handful of houses clustered loosely around a larger, two-story building that was a combined blacksmith shop and general store.

It was late in the afternoon when Riot and Thaddeus rode into the settlement on two borrowed government mules. They turned the animals over to the man at the blacksmith shop and Thaddeus said, "Roslyn will be stayin' with the Barstows. I'll go see her." He hesitated, standing stoop-shouldered and weary with sorrow in the dust outside the smith's. "You comin'?"

"I'm going to buy a horse." Riot took his saddlebags off his shoulder and held them in his hand, "Listen, Thaddeus. You McCallisters were the most family I ever had." He unbuttoned one pocket of the bags and took a little money from it. "You'll be needing some cash to start fixing the place up again. This maybe'll help some." He stuck the small amount of money into his jacket pocket and held the saddlebags out to Thaddeus.

The other man shook his head. "No. I've been thinkin' on the way over here. I'm not goin' to build the place back up. At least not for a time."

"That's what your folks'd want."

"Maybe. You leavin' directly?"

"Soon's I got something to ride. And a rifle." Riot shifted his weight uncomfortably.

Thaddeus was becoming even more ill at ease than Riot, and watching him, Riot felt for the first and only time a hostility in the man's eyes. Thaddeus said, "I hope you have yourself a time, Riot. I hope you squeeze in a couple of lifetimes of high livin'."

"Take care of Roslyn." Riot touched him on the shoulder and turned back toward the blacksmith shop with no more words.

It was sunset when Riot was outfitted and ready to go. He decided he couldn't leave without saying good-by to Roslyn. He'd told her he would see her. After asking which house was the Barstow home, he rode his pinto gelding to it and dismounted to knock at the door.

An older woman answered it and, without speaking, motioned Riot into a small parlor where Roslyn and Thaddeus were seated. Then the woman disappeared into another room.

Roslyn looked up at Riot, her eyes hollow and her face lined heavily with tears that couldn't be held back. "Riot," she said, "we've been arguing. Will you help me?"

"No argument," Thaddeus said stubbornly. "Nothin' more to say."

"He's going after Blood Shirt all by himself. He's even got some wild idea about trying to destroy the cache of rifles in Mexico. He'll get himself killed!"

"Roslyn," Riot said slowly. "I can't stop him." He paused. "I wouldn't know what to say to stop him, because I got the same idea he has. All I can do is join him."

The girl leaned forward, her hands hiding her face, and cried almost silently. It was somehow far worse than wailing or hysteria. Thaddeus stood up and said softly, "I'm sorry, Roslyn."

Riot stepped forward and kneeled on one knee before the girl. He searched for words but found none. Finally he said, "He'll be back," and touched her on the wrist as he spoke. Then he stood up. "Now's the best time to go," he told Thaddeus. "Ride by night and rest by day.

Let's go get you outfitted."

By the first light of the evening star they rode out of the settlement together, Thaddeus now mounted on a good black mare with new horse furniture, and carrying a new Winchester .73 identical to the one Riot had bought.

As they left the lights of the settlement and moved into the endless dark of the prairie before them, Thaddeus said, "I'm beholden to you for what you're doin', Riot."

"No, you're not," said Riot. "And there's a couple of things I want to say. Remember the dead man you ran across four weeks ago, before you stopped and picked me up?"

"Yes."

"I left him to die. I've never claimed to be any good, and I've liked it that way. What we're doing right now seems a good idea, and maybe the only thing to do. But don't count on me too much. I want to live like hell, and go out with a bang. Any minute I may decide to stop chasing Blood Shirt, in favor of chasing some red-headed dancehall girl instead."

Thaddeus pushed his hat back and scratched his head. "That's understandable."

Two days later they rode into Fort Davis.

"If Colonel Blacker is here, it'll be worth while talkin' to him," Thaddeus said as they guided their horses across the compound. "Maybe he can give us some idea where t'start looking."

Colonel Blacker saw them almost as soon as they were announced. He'd known the McCallister family, and he told Thaddeus, "This country can't afford that kind of a loss."

"Reason we stopped in," Thaddeus told him, "we're wonderin' if you got any idea where Blood Shirt's headed just now."

"Headed south, last I heard. Lieutenant Salters tried to follow him from your ranch, but lost him inside of twenty-four hours. Right now, he might be headed south still, or east, west or north or any direction in between."

"Thing to do," Riot said, "is try to find that bunch of guns in Mexico. Blood Shirt'll be after them sooner or later."

"What do you know about those guns?" Blacker asked.

"Just that I've heard they're waiting down there somewhere."

"That's the trouble. A thousand rumors, but nobody knows anything. Those Spensers could be only in Blood Shirt's imagination."

Riot said, "The Spensers he's been shooting in my direction make too big holes to be imagination."

Blacker sat on the edge of his desk. "Yes. Quite." He bit his lower lip thoughtfully. "I believe the story to be true, so much so that I suggested the Army try to buy back those guns, at twice their cost if necessary. The Comancheros don't care who they sell them to, as long as they make money. But my suggestion was turned down. To buy back its own stolen arms, I'm told, is beneath the dignity of the Army." He looked at them sharply. "I hold you both to silence on that." He went to a map on his wall that took in Mexico down to Monterrey. "Lieutenant Salters brought back the personal effects of the Comanches, and there was one thing I noted. Five of the Indians, that is to say about half of Blood Shirt's warriors, had small pocket mirrors that I know were made here" — he pointed to a spot on the map — "in Chihuahua." Going to his desk, he opened a drawer and took a small, round mirror from it. The mirror was a simple piece of glass with a band of metal running around its edge. The back of it was painted red. "That's one of them," Blacker said. "It might mean nothing. But if I were you two young men, I'd make my way toward Chihuahua.

"As a matter of fact, I hold you to silence on our entire conversation. It's off the record and between gentlemen who have . . . had experiences with the Comanches. Officially, all I'd be able to tell you is that the Indian situation is improving rapidly and that you should leave these matters up to duly organized fighting forces. If anyone asks, that's what I've told you."

"Thank you, sir." Thaddeus stood up.

Before the two men went out of the office door, Colonel Blacker said one more thing: "Good hunting."

They rode south from the fort and then southeast into the wide, vast country where brown, swelling prairie rolled endlessly to the horizon. For more than three weeks they cross-tracked the flatlands, exploring with special care the few ridges, just below the skyline, where Comanches preferred to travel. Twice in the bitter, determined search, they ran across Indians, but the first band was a peaceful family of Coyoteros, and the second, though Comanche, was a hunting party of four old men from the Menomini tribe. The four hunters were furious because Blood Shirt had visited their tribe two weeks before and talked most of the young warriors into going with him. But they did not know where he was now.

Finally Thaddeus said, "We could spend a hundred years out in this goddam big land and not find anything. Let's go on into Alpine, and cut straight out for the Rio Grande from there."

"I might not be welcome in Alpine. They chased me out of there."

"What for?"

Riot tilted his head in a faint shrug. "Well, I won some money from a few fellows in a game of stud."

"They ran you out for that?"

"Well, not exactly. Some damned loud-mouthed ex-cardsharp claimed I was dealin' a marked deck." Riot shook his head thoughtfully. "There's nothing worse in this world than a fellow who's reformed from his evil ways."

"So they ran you out because they thought you were cheatin' at cards?"

"Well, no. They didn't get too sore about that. But that ex-gambler and me had a hell of an argument before long, you see, and so they chased me out of town along with some saddle-tramp they thought was a friend of mine, though I'd never seen him before in my life."

"Since when are they chasin' a man out of town for arguing with a fellow?"

"Well, this particular fellow, I shot."

"Oh." Thaddeus nodded. "Well, that makes it a little clearer."

Riot leaned forward and stroked his pinto's black mane. "I'm all in favor of going through Alpine. But just in case they haven't cooled down yet, let's be ready to go through fairly fast."

They got to the town at six o'clock on a baking hot evening. It was suppertime, and few people were about as they rode down a street fetlock deep in wispy, light dust that erupted in small, separate clouds under their horses' hoofs.

At the first corner they reached there was a hostelry with a saloon directly across from it. They rode into the stables and Riot told the old man on duty to feed the horses six quarts of grain apiece. "But leave their saddles on for an hour," he added. "If we're not back by then, you can strip them."

They crossed the thick dust of the street, and Riot touched his gunbutt lightly to make sure the revolver was in just the right position before he pushed through the doors under a sign that read, *Ace In The Hole Saloon.*

Behind him, Thaddeus touched his gun too, unconscious of his imitation of Riot, before following him through the batwing doors.

The Ace in The Hole was a small, tough place with a worn oak bar and rough frame walls that were hung with calendars and tintypes, most of which showed pretty girls who were not overly dressed.

There were eight or ten men in the bar, four of them playing cards at a table, the others scattered in groups along the counter. The barman glanced up as Riot entered, and Riot said, "How's tricks, Zed?"

Zed paused as the other men in the room glanced casually at the two men coming in, then turned back to what they were doing. Taking his cue from the general mood of indifference, Zed advanced to meet Riot and Thaddeus as they approached the other side of the bar. "Things're quiet. Not much doin'. Whisky?"

Riot nodded. "Was thinking maybe the fellows around here'd be sore about that shooting."

Pouring shots of whisky with an expert twist of the wrist, the barman shrugged. "That was a long time ago. Around Alpine we always say forgive and forget."

Riot raised his glass. "Well, here's to sweet charity!" Out of the corner of his eye, he saw one of the men at the end of the bar wipe his mouth with the back of his sleeve and go out the door. "In about ten minutes we'll know whether the other good people in Alpine agree with Zed and these men in here." He spoke low, his head turned toward Thaddeus.

"We coulda swung around the town," Thaddeus whispered. "We could get out right now."

"I was thinking that same thing, about going around. Was thinkin' it for an hour before we got here. But damn it, it's been so long since

I've tasted this fine liquid refreshment that a lynch mob seems trivial alongside it."

Thaddeus drank his whisky and put the glass down. "I could never get too enthused about the stuff." His face was still somber. "Besides, this ain't why I'm traveling."

"You just ain't been broke in proper. For it to do you any real good, you got to cooperate with it. Drink a lot so's it'll have a fair chance." Riot put a banknote on the counter and said, "Take out the bottle, Zed." He poured fresh drinks for them both, then walked to the front of the saloon where one small window gave him a view of the street and the corner.

Thaddeus followed him and stood by, drinking slowly but conscientiously from the glass. "Anything?"

"Not yet."

"What about that fellow leanin' against the wall across the street there?"

"He's no lynch mob. He's a fellow who's been cooperating with a bottle of Missouri Mule above and beyond the call of duty."

In the half-hour they waited, Riot pulled far ahead of Thaddeus in amount of liquor consumed. But the slower drinker was beginning to feel a certain hollowness in his head.

"I guess it's okay," Riot said at last. "Let's go on to bigger things. This ain't the best place in

Alpine to spend a pleasant evening."

"What I think, I think we oughtta get ourselves a good supper, a good sleep and a good breakfast. After that we could take off for Presidio feelin' fine."

"Damned good idea! But we best bear in mind that Presidio and the Rio Grande are a long, miserable ride away from here. So we owe it to ourselves to leave not only refreshed in body, but in mind and spirit as well."

"That stuff makes you talk pretty fancy." Thaddeus went back to the bar and put down his now empty glass. "I gotta get somethin' to eat."

Riot put his own glass on the bar. Picking up his change to stuff into his pocket, and still carrying the now half-empty bottle, he said, "So long, Zed."

"Riot," the barman said, "they're forgivin' and forgettin', but they kinda got you on probation. You go too far, and they'll still hang ya."

"No trouble," Riot grinned. "I love everybody in Alpine. Even you, you ugly barkeep."

Zed shook his head and Riot and Thaddeus went out onto the street. At the corner, Riot stopped to take a drink and offered the bottle to Thaddeus, who said, "Thanks, no."

"So you want to eat?"

"Yeah."

"Best place for eatin' is the Bird Cage up the way here. It's also a good place to keep out of trouble."

"I'll bet." Thaddeus fell in beside Riot and they crossed the street.

"You'll bet what?" Riot took another pull at the rapidly emptying bottle.

"I'll bet the Bird Cage is a good place to keep out of trouble."

Riot considered this for a time. Then he said, "You could lose your shirt makin' bets like that."

The Bird Cage was a big, colorful place filled with constant movement, unlike anything Thaddeus had ever seen. Piano music was coming from somewhere out of sight behind the mass of people before them as Riot and Thaddeus pushed into the place. The huge, single room was lighted by one large, crystal-decorated chandelier that hung in stately beauty from the high ceiling. Thaddeus guessed there must be about two hundred people in the place, and about every third or fourth person was a girl, although plenty of them were old enough to be called women without fear of insulting them. They were dressed in pretty clothes, and even their shoes were pretty fragile things with tall, slender heels.

Riot said, "What's the matter?"

"Nothin'. They sure got those dresses low-cut in front."

"Umm." Riot gently pulled Thaddeus away from the doorway. "You ever been in a dive like this?"

"Nope. Was goin' to go into one with Ed in Pecos once, but we didn't have the time."

"For this sort of thing, boy, you make the time. This is an important part of living the good, full life. Come on."

Riot pushed a way through the crowd to his right, away from the bar, and they passed gambling tables that were surrounded by intense, sometimes laughing men and women. They came to a few tables along one wall of the Bird Cage and took chairs at one of them.

Thaddeus thought a few of the people who'd noticed Riot had recognized him, and now, as a waiter came to their table, he realized that a lot of attention was being paid to them. The games didn't stop, and none of the men approached, but at least fifty pairs of eyes were unblinkingly resting on them.

"Bring us a couple of whopping big steaks," Riot told the waiter, putting his bottle on the table. "And bring us two glasses and another bottle. This one isn't holding out too well."

"No more for me," Thaddeus said as the waiter disappeared. "I'd be in trouble for sure."

Riot ignored him and filled both of the glasses as soon as they were on the table. "Thaddeus is too much name. Mind if I chop it down to Tad?"

"Don't give a damn."

"Good. Let's drink on it."

Thaddeus turned the name Tad over in his mind as he drank to the christening. The McCallisters had cut down all his brothers' names, but somehow they'd left his whole. "I like that name fine," he decided aloud. "Good, simple sound to it." The drinks were coming easier now, and he wondered why he'd ever thought he wouldn't be able to control the whisky, no matter how much of it he drank. There was nothing to it. After a time, he said, "Thaddeus is more dignified. I'll go back to that name when I'm sixty years old."

Riot nodded affably. "Here's to sixty!"

An almost physical pain went through Tad as the full impact of living to sixty became clear to him. There were a lot of things he'd wanted to tell Riot, but he hadn't been able to find the right words. Now, he realized, there was no reason to hold back. All he had to do was say things straightforwardly, yet with tact and understanding.

"You poor sonofabitch, Riot." He held his glass toward the other man, his face creased with lines of concern. "You'll be dead before snow flies."

Riot tipped his glass and drank. Then he nodded. "Ain't it a shame! A cryin' shame. Poor old Riot. So many card games. So many fights. So many women and so much whisky. He's goin' to have to go like hell to get in his share!"

The waiter brought their steaks, good-sized chunks of well-cooked beef, and Riot said, "This is the place to spend time. The Bird Cage. A man can get anything he wants in here, if he's got the money to pay for it."

"Anything?"

"Yep. They'll even send down to the Chinese place in the alley and get you a smoke of opium, if you want it, and you can rent a room upstairs to smoke it in. Anything."

Between bites of the steak, Tad said glumly, "Anything, maybe, except a longer life." He swallowed hard and stopped eating as emotion crowded into him, and he realized with strangely mingled shame and indifference that his eyes were filling with tears. "Jesus! You and Roslyn was the only ones left. The only ones! And it makes me feel awful bad that you'll be gone pretty quick, too. Life's a crazy, hard thing to figure out. Things happen —"

When he trailed off, Riot said, "Just between us, there's one very good thing about all this dyin' business." He held his palms up briefly. "You don't worry. There's nothin' to worry about. You can do whatever you damn well want, and that's a nice feelin'."

"I always thought you did pretty much what ya wanted to anyhow."

"Not full scale." Riot shook his head. "You don't understand what I mean, Tad." Glancing around the room, frowning, he said, "How can I explain it to you? Ah, I got it! Now, Tad, you see that fellow with the handlebar over there at the roulette table?"

"Mean-lookin' fellow?"

"That's him. Now you, an' me, an' most any-body sees a fellow like him from time to time. An' you hate him the minute you lay eyes on 'im. Right?"

"Yeah!" Tad said firmly. "He's got a nasty look 'bout him. Squinty eyes, and a mean mouth. An' he's watchin' us like he don't like us no more'n we like him."

"Well now, bein' normal, easy goin' boys, we just look at 'im and say ugg to ourselves. Long as he doesn't cross us, we live an' let live. Right?"

"Right."

Riot tapped his thumb against his chest. "But it's different with me. Since I ain't goin' to be around long anyhow, I got a feelin' of freedom. Show ya what I mean."

Getting up from the table, Riot walked over to the roulette game. Standing before the mustached man, he said, "Mister, I do not like you at all." Then he hit him with a long, looping right and the man landed on the roulette table, scattering chips in all directions, rolled over once and fell off the far side. Amid screams and curses and people grabbing wildly for chips on the floor, Riot walked back and sat down. "Now, you see what I'm tryin' to say, Tad?"

"Yep." The whole thing seemed perfectly logical to Tad.

A ragged line of about five husky men pushed through the room and stood facing the two men. A short, beefy man with a cigar stub clenched between his teeth said, "You shouldn't oughtta hit my customers that way, Riot."

Riot grinned happily. "It's all right, Bush. I was just explainin' a thing to my friend here."

"What'n hell'dya hit 'im for?"

"He had a mean look about 'im," Tad said.

"Huh?" Bush stared at Tad curiously, then folded heavy arms over his chest. "We'll jus' wait here until the dealer gets his count. If the house comes out behind, Riot, you're gonna have to make good."

Riot cut a piece of steak and said, "Eat, Tad.

May not be much time later on."

The excitement at the roulette table was dying down as they finished their steaks. There were no more chips on the floor, and the players were crowding around once more, ready to bet on the bouncing ball. The man Riot had hit was being pacified by two of his friends who gestured toward the table where Riot and Tad were sitting surrounded by Bush and his men, and evidently the two friends convinced him that Riot was already in enough trouble. He glared furiously at Riot, then went angrily back to his place at the roulette table.

The horseman on the wheel came over and said to Bush, "I got the chips stacked up again. Figure the house come out about five hundred to the good."

"All right. Then I ain't mad, Riot." Bush held a match to his stub of cigar. "But mind your manners, or next time it'll go hard on you."

Riot stood up and grinned, his eyes beginning to dance. "Why, Bush, you're threatenin' me!"

"You're damn right I am." The Bird Cage owner turned around and started away, his four muscular employees following him.

Riot left ten dollars on the table for the steaks and whisky, and with Tad behind him, moved away. Tad thought they were leaving, but Riot stopped at the same roulette table before the same man.

"I still don't like you," Riot said, and he knocked him over the roulette table again.

This time there was no good humor left in anyone. Instead of going for the chips, they turned on Riot, on each other, on anyone who pushed against them. A big man on the far side of the table who had been placing a bet just as Riot's victim came rolling over the table yelled, "Can't a man lose his money in peace!" He put big, work-calloused hands under the table, heaved, and the whole roulette game was up-ended.

Bush roared, "Everybody stand still! Just a misunderstandin'!" But his booming voice was lost in the greater avalanche of noise that swept through the Bird Cage. He turned in time to see Riot flattening the mean-faced man's two companions, and yelled to his four bouncers, "Whatever else, break that man up! I'll get you, Riot!" He screeched the name Riot, and a prospector picked up the word gleefully.

At the top of his leathery lungs the prospector screamed, "Riot! Riot!" In a burst of enthusiasm, he kicked over a poker table in front of him. "And a damn good'un, too!"

Riot saw the four professional toughs coming

at him, and he hit the first one so hard he almost tore his head off. Then Riot charged across an open space, jumped to a chuck-a-luck table and from there jumped even higher to catch the bottom of the chandelier. He yelled, "Look out beneath!" as he and the chandelier came crashing down from the ceiling and the room was plunged into shadowed darkness.

As Riot leaped for the chandelier, Tad had seen the mean-looking man pull a gun and aim at the flying figure. Tad's body wasn't behaving as well as it might, but he pulled his own revolver and brought the barrel down over the man's head before the lights went out.

A moment later Riot was at his side. "Jesus, Tad!" Riot jerked him over toward a wall. "Never stand around in the middle of a free-for-all like that. Things can come at you from anyplace!" Riot grabbed a bottle from a table in the half-light along part of the wall and took a drink, then tossed the bottle lightly through a window nearby. As the glass shattered, a man came bulling out from the dark room and butted Riot hard in the chest. A fiery shock of pain enveloped Riot and he slumped back against the wall as the man reared back for another running charge. Tad stepped forward and brought his fist up in a wide uppercut that caught the man on the side of the head and sent him crashing into a nearby corner where some girls squealed in delighted fear. The man stayed in the corner.

Turning to Riot, Tad said, "You okay?"

"Will be. Give me a second."

Suddenly almost sober, Tad put one arm in front of Riot and turned to protect him against whatever might come. Two rassling men, trying to bear-hug each other to death, wobbled grimly toward the wall, and Tad put up one foot and braced his back against the wall, then pushed out with his foot and sent both men sailing out into the darkness of the Bird Cage. "You better yet?" he whispered anxiously. "That smack on the chest . . . it didn't do real damage?"

After a small hesitation, Riot said, "No, no. I'm comin' around."

Tad started walking Riot along the wall and toward the door. A cowboy dived head first through a window ahead of them, without bothering to open it, and moonlight played into the room. A girl who had somehow lost the top half of her dress ran through the pale light, and right behind her ran a howling man who had the missing part of her clothing in his extended hand and seemed to be offering to give it back to her.

A fist came from nowhere and slammed Tad

on the ear, pounding his head against the wall, and then the fist and its owner were gone in the surrounding confusion.

Shaking his head, Tad said, "We're gettin' there. Be at the front door in a minute."

Bush had set himself up at the front door, hoping to keep looting down to a minimum. A drunken assortment of men in the Bird Cage had pledged themselves to be his unwanted assistants. At the cry of, "Riot!" one of them had voiced the opinion of all concerned by saying, "Oh, my God! We gotta save the whisky!" Hopping over the bar, they'd started out with as many bottles as they could carry. Bush had managed to stop some of them. Others, he had not. Now he'd started shooting to back up his suggestions that they cease helping him.

In front of Riot and Tad a shadowy, formless figure of a man lurched out the door and crossed the boardwalk to the street holding a bottle high over his head. Bush just outside the door, yelled, "Hold it, God damn it!"

The drunk raised the bottle and started drinking at the same time that Bush started shooting. The third wild shot shattered the bottle in the drunk's hands with such violence that he sat down hard in the street. Staring at the bottle neck he still held in his hand, he muttered with reverence, "God, what whisky!"

Riot and Tad were out of the door when Bush turned around and saw them in the dim light coming from other buildings.

"You!" Bush said to Riot, his voice not quite under control. "You —"

Tad was training his gun on Bush as he helped Riot along the boardwalk. "Just keep holdin' your gun at your side that way, Mr. Bush."

"That is his fault! My place is wrecked!" Bush kept his gun pointed down at the ground, but he balled his free hand into a tight fist and waved it. "I'll have his hide for this!"

Riot was coming around fast now. He stood up straight, not needing Tad's supporting arm any more. "My hide," he told Bush, "is a collector's item. Better men than you have been after it for years."

They were at a corner now, and Riot said, "Duck around and run." He shot twice into the dirt at Bush's feet and hurried around the corner after the other. About fifty feet along the dark street there were two horses tied to a hitching rail.

"We use them?" Tad asked.

"Hell no, the evenin's young yet!" Riot untied the animals, listening intently. Soon, over the dimmer thunder of the fight in the Bird Cage, he heard running feet. Then he yelled,

"Wahoo!" in a high, loud voice and slapped the animal nearest him over the rump. Both horses galloped away toward the open country beyond the street, and Riot grabbed Tad and pushed him into the pitch-black shadows between two darkened buildings.

Bush ran around the corner with several Bird Cage hired hands behind him. Bush could hear the retreating horses, and he bellowed, "They're gettin' away!" He fired at the fading hoofbeats and, sputtering with fury, said, "Get horses! We'll go after 'em!"

Within half a minute Bush and his men were galloping out along the street on hastily re-cruited mounts. Even before they were out of sight Riot stepped out of the shadows. He shook his head and said, "Bush's got no sense of humor; that's his failin'."

Tad's head was banging as though a lazy, per-sistent demon were inside hitting it with a ham-mer. "I don't feel too good," he said. "Everything's kinda wobbly."

"What you need right away is a good shot of firewater. Clear up that punch you took on the side of the head in there."

"I'd like t'lay down an' go to sleep."

"Nope. Can't give in to temptation that way, Tad. It's a weak man's way out. You got to be firm." Riot led him down the alley to a door.

There were a few men scattered in various prone positions around it, and Riot said, "This is the back door to the Bird Cage."

Tad pulled back and Riot's hand fell from his shoulder. "But we just come outa there! They don't like us in there no more!"

"Come on! It'll be just for a minute!" Riot grabbed him again by the shoulder and Tad went along, grumbling thickly.

They passed through a storeroom before coming to the big main room, which was still dark. There were a few sounds of scuffling here and there, and an occasional grunt of pain, but the fight had almost died out. Riot lit a match.

A girl and a man were cozily seated behind the piano to his right, where they'd evidently weathered out the brawl. Riot dropped the match and went to the piano. "Say, lady, do you —"

"Get your own girl," the man said sullenly.

"I just want —"

The man stood up, a belligerent shadow against the wall. He raised his fist and felt a cool, small, smoothness touching his upper lip lightly.

"That," Riot said, "is a gunmuzzle. Shut up! Now, miss, do you know what happened to Annie?"

"Annie Firefly?"

"That's right."

"She's workin' at Ma Minette's place. She went on over there last week as a four-dollar girl. She's doin' great these days!"

"Thanks."

Riot turned to leave, and with an effort Tad struggled along beside him. A bartender at the far end of the big room worked up the nerve to light a lamp as they were going out the back door, and by the glimmering light, Riot saw an unbroken bottle lying on its side. He picked it up and jiggled it, testing its weight. "Third full," he announced happily.

In the alley, Riot walked on to the next street and started down it. He passed the bottle to Tad and said, "This'll take the stumble outa that walk of yours."

"It'll kill me."

"It'll damn near kill you, but at the same time it'll buck you up. Try it."

Tad took a shot, and he did feel better — or didn't notice the pain so much. Riot swallowed some liquid from the bottle, and they walked on.

"Where we goin'?"

"Minette's. Annie's there. She's half Paiute, cute as a new five-dollar gold piece and a hell of a woman. She and me's friends." Riot glanced at Tad uncertainly. He said, "There's a couple pretty girls at Minette's. But when you look at Minette herself, try to close one eye and squint through the other. She's no ravin' beauty."

Tad heard horses and pulled Riot closer to the shadow of a nearby building, afraid it might be Bush and his men searching the town. The riders went on by, and he said, "Oughtn't we get us the hell out of town, Riot? Bush is awful mad about his place."

"Nah." Riot waved the idea away. "He always sees the dark side of things first."

"Maybe he's still seein' the dark side."

"Tad, with a girl like Annie half a block away, you just don't leave town. It ain't done. Come on!"

Minette was a heavy, rock-jawed woman with the marks of smallpox on her face. She let them into a simply furnished parlor with several chairs along the walls, and Riot said, "I come to see Annie Firefly."

There was a delighted shriek from a room beyond at the sound of his voice, and a young, pretty girl with dark hair and copper-tinted cheeks rushed into the parlor wearing a flaming-red kimono. "Riot!" she shouted.

"Please!" Minette said haughtily. "This is a whorehouse which has got some dignity, Annie!" She turned to Tad. "And you, sir? I'll bring out some of the girls. I think you might like Nellie."

"Give him anything he wants, Minette," Riot said, still not quite sure what to do with Tad. "He's a personal friend of me and Dave Bush."

Riot and Annie left the room, and Tad said, "Please, ma'am, if it's all the same to you, could I jus' sit in one of these chairs and rest."

Minette frowned with disapproval. "Well, if that's all you're up to."

"Just now, that's all I'm up to." Tad tried to make it sound as though normally he was up to all sorts of mysterious and intriguing things. "Just now."

Tad sat down and fell asleep almost immediately. It was a fitful sleep, and he was vaguely aware of fairly heavy traffic in the parlor and an occasional giggle. Then someone was shaking his shoulder and he looked up to see Riot grinning down at him. "Ma Minette says you exhausted every girl in the house."

"You ready to go?"

"Any time you are."

It was still and quiet outside, and the streets were haunted with dim starlight. They walked in silence back to the stable where they'd left their horses. On the way, Riot snapped his fingers and said, "Almost forgot. You wanted to get a good night's sleep and a good breakfast.

How you feel about those items now?"

"I just want to get outa Alpine before they lynch us both."

"I'm with you."

A sleepy young boy was on duty at the hostelry now and he took a night's board for both horses and helped them get the animals ready. "Ya see the excitement earlier?"

"What excitement?" Riot drew the cinch strap up around his pony's stomach.

"There was a really freewheelin', devil-take-the-hindmost badman in town tonight. Name of Riot Holiday. Riot at the Bird Cage. You missed out on it?" The boy shook his head sadly for them. "They was gonna hang him from the rafters in Leary's stable, but foun' out they had the wrong man. They almost hung ol' Whit Sweeney instead, jus' because they found 'im under a chandelier ol' Holiday tore outa the ceiling at the Bird Cage. Dave Bush and a posse's been out lookin' for 'im most the night. They say he keeps goin', he'll have one of the biggest names in the whole country."

"Names as what?" Riot asked.

The boy patted the pinto. "As a badman, 'course. Like Clay Allison an' Jesse James an' all them. Killed himself a man right here in Alpine not long ago."

When Riot and Tad rode toward the door of

the stable, Riot heard hoofbeats of several horses coming into town and he pulled his reins, forcing Tad and his black horse out of line of the door and the street beyond.

Bush and his men rode by with two riderless horses. "Wouldn't have had t'chase them cayuses all night if we'd just stopped shootin' at 'em," one man complained.

"They could be in Canada by now," another grumbled.

As the men rode by, the boy was watching Riot and Tad with a puzzled expression. Then he said, "Why didn't you want 'em t'see you?"

"Never ask that kind of question and you'll maybe reach a ripe old age," Riot told him. "But for just now — ten years from now you can tell your kids Riot Holiday once flipped you a dollar." He flipped a silver coin to the boy. The youngster gasped and Riot and Tad rode out of Alpine.

It was still night when they camped some distance south of the town. "Guess we could both use some shuteye," Riot said as he eased his head back into his saddle.

But Tad was already out and breathing heavily.

They slept soundly, not yet knowing what the morning would bring.

The Third Month

6

Riot opened his eyes when the sky was blue-gray and the sun was not yet pushing up over the hills to the east. He had coffee boiling over a low, almost smokeless fire when Tad sat up and groaned, clutching at his head.

"Coffee'll dilute that brain shellac," Riot said cheerfully. "You won't die."

"I'd just as soon."

The coffee didn't perk Tad up. He grew more glum and serious with each sip of the hot black liquid.

"Somethin' eating you?" Riot asked him.

"Yeah."

"What?"

Tad stared at Riot over the top of the tin cup. "You an' me have reached a partin' of the ways, Riot."

"What'n hell you talking about?"

"Just what I said. I been thinkin' about it. Last night, ridin' out of Alpine; this mornin', since I been awake. I'm sorry about it. Damn sorry. But that's the way it is."

Riot finished his coffee and tossed the grounds at the bottom of the cup into the fire. "You're crazy — or still drunk."

"Nope. Neither one. Standin' over my folks there in the house, I promised myself to do a thing, or at least to do my best to do it. But where was I last night? Out drinkin' and fightin' and tearin' around. And the dirt on their graves not yet settled!"

"Well, what's wrong with that? You can't just plain stop living. And you didn't go near them girls!"

Tad shrugged, still nursing his coffee. "Don't matter. Thing is, I can see the way you like t'live. Wouldn't care much for it, for a steady diet, myself. But that ain't here or there. You like it, and on you maybe it looks good. But it don't fit me. Especially now." Tad frowned, searching for words. "Not only does it take up time, but a fellow can get killed foolin' around that way. And I can't afford to get killed just now."

"Then what's this talk about splitting up?"

"I'll go down to Chihuahua and do what I

95

can toward riddin' this world of Blood Shirt and them rifles. You go an' have yourself a fling, while you can. How's your chest?"

"It's okay, but it doesn't take kindly to being slugged, for damn sure." Riot got up and started to break camp. "We got a long way to go."

Tad threw his coffe grains on the dying fire, using the same twist of the wrist as Riot had used. "*I* got a long way to go."

"Listen, idiot," Riot said, without real anger, "I got a grudge here, too. Not like you, 'cause I was no blood kin, but still it's a pretty powerful feelin' in me. Besides, I promised Roslyn you'd be back. You're all the family she's got now. And you'd get yourself killed in no time, going on by yourself. You just don't have no know-how. So stop arguin', and let's get going!"

Tad stood up and put the coffee cup down on a rock beside him. "I'm travelin' alone."

"You want your head busted?"

"You want your chest walloped?"

Riot studied him for a minute, then threw his saddle over the pinto. "You wouldn't hit me in the chest if you could."

"Like hell!"

"Will you stop jabberin'?"

Tad strode over to where Riot was bent down, reaching under the paint for the cinch. He said, "I mean it!" and pulled Riot up and around.

96

Riot brought his fist up as Tad spun him around, and the fist caught Tad on the point of the jaw and sent him sailing back and over the rock where he'd placed his cup.

The cup clinked onto the ground beside him, and not quite understanding why he did it, Tad got up and very carefully replaced the cup before stepping toward Riot again. "This time," he said, "I'll clobber you right over that arrowhead!"

"Hah!" Riot sneered. "I'll prove to your own face you're a damned liar!" He held his hands far out at his sides. "There's your target! Hit me right next to the Bull Durham package in the shirt pocket!"

Tad swung hard and caught Riot squarely in the mouth.

Riot saw the fist coming and rocked back, cutting down on the force of the blow. But still, he had been struck hard, and went back against the pinto. The yet uncinched saddle slid off the paint's back onto the ground.

Riot regained his balance and stood still, running his tongue over his teeth to test them. Then he said, "Tad, you ain't got a chance in hell, fighting me. You must know that."

"I'm going on alone!" Tad braced himself, pulled back his right arm and hit Riot again.

They were almost evenly matched for size

and weight. What Riot had in coordination, speed and power, Tad made up for in sheer desperation. Riot shook off Tad's second punch and knocked him to the ground with a swift, chopping left, and Tad got up and rushed him, trying to throw him to the ground.

"You dumb cowpoke!" Riot panted. "I coulda broke your jaw, you barrelin' in wide open like!"

Straining to throw the other man, Tad said nothing. Riot's left foot bumped against a small, firmly imbedded rock, and the two men slammed to the ground with Tad on top. Riot grunted as Tad's falling weight crunched against his chest, and he went weak for an instant. Then his strength flowed back and he muttered, "I'm annoyed now," and broke loose his right arm and clouted Tad on the jaw with his elbow.

Tad held on grimly, shaking his head to clear it, and the elbow hit him again with the force of a mule's kick. He changed tactics, reared back onto his knees and started swinging. Twice he hit Riot and once he hit a rock when Riot ducked.

With more room to work in, Riot arched upward with a full-sized swing that landed on the side of Tad's head and sent him rolling away. Both men got up at the same time and circled each other.

"You oughtta give up before you get hurt," Riot advised. "I could whip you with one hand tied behind me."

Breathing heavily, Tad said, "No McCallister was ever beat easy."

"You admit it's just a matter of time!"

"Hell I do!" Tad stepped closer suddenly and began to throw punches.

Riot ducked, came in and under and sank his left fist into Tad's stomach. His right fist came up as Tad's head jerked down and the two chunks of solid-boned flesh cracked together savagely. Somehow Tad managed to stay on his feet, still swinging at Riot with strength but no accuracy. A wildly careening left bounced off of Riot's chest and the man almost doubled up, stepping back quickly to sit on the rock beside Tad's coffee cup. Following the left with a wild, looping right that hummed through the air, Tad threw himself off balance and, half out on his feet, he went sprawling onto the ground.

Gasping for breath, Riot watched Tad as he sat up and slowly rubbed a hand with bleeding knuckles across his bruised face. "You are pretty tough," Riot managed to say. "I never saw a fellow knock himself down so hard before."

Tad gathered his feet under him and got to his feet. He started rubbing sand and dirt off of his torn knuckles and said, "Very comical. I wouldn't exactly say you won that fight."

"Win it? I wasn't even in it. Just sittin' here watching you kick hell out of yourself."

"I'm sorry I hit your goddam chest."

"I'm sorry you did, too. That chest sure is my Achilles' heel." Riot stood up, gritted his teeth and stretched his shoulders a little. "Like getting shot with an arrow all over again." He rubbed his right fist in his left palm. "Well, shall we fight some more?"

"I ain't got the time t'stand around fightin' you all week!"

"Well then, let's go."

Tad stood still for a few seconds, thinking. Then he took a deep breath and went over to start making up his saddleroll.

Riding by day now that there was no immediate threat of running into Blood Shirt unexpectedly, they got halfway to Presidio without speaking more than two words at a time. One afternoon they saw a mother grizzly nearly half a mile away moving between two clumps of trees, three cubs following in a line after her. As the mother bear disappeared in the trees the third cub in line reared on the second cub, put itself out of balance and rolled onto its side.

"Must be named Thaddeus," Riot remarked.

A full five minutes later, Tad's wide mouth

broke into a grin. He turned to Riot and said, "You're a no-good bastard." After that he started to laugh, and he laughed until it almost choked him, and Riot got to chuckling, too.

Moving down the main street of Presidio, the two men swung their horses out to bypass a small cart pulled by a lazy-stepping, forlorn donkey. Not far before them, they could see the wide Rio Grande rolling slowly by the edge of the border town.

"Been here before?" Tad asked.

"Nope." Riot spotted a blacksmith shop and said, "We ought to get our horses' shoes checked, buy a few supplies."

"Yeah."

Riot turned his horse into the hitching-rail before the shop. There was a small general store next door, and after they'd bought grain, grease, coffee and salt, plus a few pounds of charqui and bannock, they took the stuff to the shop and put it in their now stripped traveling gear.

Riot straightened up after packing his share of supplies. "Oughtta hold the old warbag a while. The smith'll take some time with the shoeing, Tad. Would you start swinging at me if I offered to buy you a drink?"

"Guess one wouldn't hurt — much."

They walked down the dusty street and into the nearest bar. The saloon was small and dark, despite the brilliant late-afternoon sun on the street outside, and there were many flies on the counter.

They were starting on their second glasses, Tad eyeing his with wary suspicion, when two tall, thin men with the built-in look of gunfighters walked softly through the doorway. The older of the two men studied the few customers in the bar with thoughtful slowness, picked Riot and Tad out of the group with his eyes, and started over, the younger man following him.

"You two fellows own the black and the pinto that're over at the smith's?"

"Why?" Riot asked.

"Oh, no special reason."

"Well then, for no special reason, that's our business."

"Don't get smart," the second man said.

"Relax, Cummings," the older man said softly. "From the looks of your horses, and your stuff — and you — it'd seem you been doin' some travelin'."

"You know any other way than traveling, to get to Presidio?"

"Mister, we don't mean to be nosy like this, but it's our job. We're Rangers."

"Well, range somewheres else," Riot suggested mildly.

"We just rode in from up north," Tad said quickly.

"Cross Commanche sign?"

"No. Nothin' much."

"Where you ridin'?"

"To Brazil," said Riot.

"Lemme teach 'im some manners," the second Ranger said.

Tad stepped between them and said, "It's okay, mister. No offense."

"You his nursemaid?"

Riot straightened up behind Tad, then relaxed, back against the bar, as Tad said, "Are you deliberately looking for a beatin'?"

"I'm lookin' not t' leave no smart alecks push no Rangers around!"

Tad stared at him briefly. He said, "You're a talker," and he turned back to the bar.

"Turn 'round," the young Ranger snarled. "I'll show you who's a talker!"

Tad turned. The Ranger threw the first punch, and they stood toe-to-toe trading blows. There was no skill in their fighting, no attempt made by either one to parry or duck. They simply swung at one another as hard and as fast as they could, neither giving ground. Slowly, as they shifted their weight with their hard-thrown fists, they circled each other, and so it was that when Tad's opponent started to weaken, the Ranger's back was to Riot. Tad struck two blows that were not returned, and on his third swing he knocked the Ranger down. The Ranger fell on his back with his head near the bar. Spitting blood he cursed and his hand went toward his gun.

Riot's foot came down with no great force on the prone man's chest, so that the sharp rowels on Riot's boot just about touched the Ranger's chin. "You touch that gun, and I'll give you a backward kick at your face."

The Ranger's hand moved away from the gunbutt quickly, and a moment later, he got to his feet. The older man walked to him. "If you'd touched that gun, Cummings, I'da likely shot you myself."

Tad walked to the bar and finished what was left of his drink. He was bleeding slightly at the corner of his lip but was all right otherwise.

Riot said, "You and your wild, wicked ways'll get us in trouble one of these days." He shook his head sadly. "Beatin' up a Texas Ranger."

The bloody young man left the saloon, and the older Ranger walked to them and said, "He thinks bein' with the outfit makes 'im one of God's favored. He's new. He'll learn."

"I did 'im a good turn," Tad said. "Otherwise,

he'd wound up fightin' Riot."

"Riot? Riot Holiday?"

"That's me."

The Ranger studied Riot with keen, steady eyes. Finally he said, "Well, sorry for troublin' you."

A thin-face Mexican watched as the Ranger walked away.

By sunset they rode out of Presidio. They crossed the Rio Grande on a small ferry and led their horses ashore on the far side of the river at Ojinaga. Mounting again, they rode into the tiny town of adobe-walled houses and mud huts. In the darkening streets, a rider approached them, and Riot remembered having seen him, the thin-faced Mexican at the saloon in Presidio.

"A word?" the man said.

Riot pulled up his pinto, his eyes darting swiftly into the shadows around them. "What about?"

"The man I work for is most anxious to meet you. He believes it might be a good thing for everyone concerned."

"Why?"

The Mexican smiled, showing two prominent gold teeth. "Because of making money."

Riot glanced at Tad and then turned back to

the Mexican. "It might be worth our while to talk. We'll watch where we're being taken, friend. And if this is a holdup, or any other damn tricky kind of thing, you won't live out the night."

The gold teeth showed again. "You can trust me."

Following a few feet behind their guide, Riot said, "Well, what do you think of Mexico?"

Tad said in a low voice, "Why we goin' with him?"

Without lowering his tone, Riot answered, "Because he looks like a crook to me. And in our line, we should get to know all the crooks we can."

At a medium-sized adobe house near the edge of Ojinaga, the Mexican stopped and got down from his horse. "We go in here."

They dismounted and tied their horses at a hitching-rail before the house, and Riot pulled his gun. "I'll just carry this in my hand a bit," he told Gold Teeth.

The man shrugged. "From your point of view, it is a wise thing."

They entered the dark house and went into a room where two other Mexicans were seated beside a low-burning lantern.

Gold Teeth said, "The man I work for," and pointed to a fat, thick-mustached Mexican with an inch of lace showing beneath the sleeves of his black coat. "And one of his – employees." The other Mexican was big and very dark and wore crossed bandoleers over his chest. A shotgun was in his arms.

The fat man waved to a couple of chairs. "Sit down, Mr. Holiday. You and your friend are welcome."

"What is it you want to talk about?" Riot asked, still standing, but replacing his gun.

"I've been trying to make a suitable contact. Perhaps you are the man I've been looking for."

"You don't know anything about me."

"You are modest, Mr. Holiday." The fat man made a small gesture with his hand. "You see, I do know a few things about you, by reputation. Also, I understand that your associate has no love for the Texas Rangers."

"Get to the point."

"You Americans must learn to relax." The fat man leaned forward in his chair. "May I speak frankly?"

"Yeah."

"Are you a thief?"

"No."

"A pity. Ah, but never mind. Would you like to make several thousand dollars a year?"

"Depends on how many thousand, and for what."

"I have a problem. I am almost always in possession of a large supply of goods that I can do very little with. Cattle, for instance. Very simply, I need someone, an American, to work with me. To take my goods north, beyond the Rio Grande, and to sell them up there at a handsome profit. I had such a man with me for some time. He averaged better than twelve thousand dollars a year. But he has retired."

"A forced retirement?"

"Quite simply, the Rangers shot him. For some time now, both the Rangers and the U.S. Army have very nearly choked off my business in the United States. They are guarding the Rio Grande very carefully. My . . . merchandise has not been getting through."

"You know why, don't you?"

"I don't follow you."

"The rifles. That's why Tad Johnson here, and me, rode down this way. With that many guns there's a lot of money to be made by a lot of people. We were hoping to get some of it."

"They'll make profit all right," Gold Teeth agreed. "Vinaro may make fifty thousand dollars."

"Be quiet," the fat one ordered. To Riot he said, "I have no rifles. But you will still be able to get rich with me."

"I'm interested in the big, quick money. Johnson and me will try to get a hand in those guns first. If that doesn't pan out, maybe we'll take you up."

"The job may not be open by then."

"I'll take my chances. Vinaro is in Chihuahua?"

The fat man's eyes grew veiled, and Riot thought he'd hit home, even when the other said, "The rifles are a thing I know nothing about. If you won't work for me, you won't work for me. There's nothing more to talk about, unless you change your mind."

"That's right. Maybe another time." Riot kept his eye on the shotgun and told Tad, "Turn around and go out of the room." Without turning around, he backed to the door Tad had left open. "I hate to turn my back on a shotgun."

And then he was gone . . .

Riding out of Ojinaga, Riot and Tad came to the Rio Conchos and followed the winding river in the general direction of Chihuahua.

"Much as I disapprove of your hell-raisin' tendencies," Riot said, "I got to admit they pay off."

"How?"

"If you hadn't busted up that green Ranger, the man with the teeth wouldn't have seen us and told his boss about us. And we wouldn't

109

have talked to him, and we wouldn't know the name Vinaro."

Tad stared ahead to where the Rio Conchos disappeared, and beyond to the moon-filled sky. The rolling, sometimes broken earth seemed to stretch toward the bottom edge of the sky forever. "Big country t'find some guns in. Some mirrors and one name don't seem much t'go on, Riot."

"Well, if you keep up your violent ways, and keep gettin' us introduced into the right circles like you did tonight, we'll have more to go on in time."

"Why'd you call me Johnson?"

"First name popped into my head. Comanches know names too. Your pa had been on that place a long time, and it's damn sure that some of those warriors — maybe even Blood Shirt himself — would recognize the name McCallister as the name belongin' to a family they massacred. This is going to be chancy enough without you keeping your family name while we're in Mexico."

They followed the Rio Conchos far south, sometimes stopping off at small Mexican villages, some of them not big enough to merit a name. Neither of them spoke Spanish, so it was almost impossible to get any kind of information, let alone ask questions, as they made their way.

At a sharp bend in the river, they came upon a half-naked Mexican boy driving a cart with huge wooden wheels that was being pulled by an ox. "Speak English?" Riot asked.

"*Sí*," the boy grinned. "Missionary school."

"Is this about where we cut off west to get to Chihuahua?"

"*Perdone?*"

"Chihuahua. *Donde es?*"

"Oh! Chihuahua ees thot way!" The boy pointed almost due west. "Steel varry far!"

"Seen many Indians around lately?"

"*Qué cosa?*"

"Indians? Comanches?"

The boy understood the word Comanches. His face lost its smiling lines and he said, "*Indios*. Yes. Come. I show you."

He left his ox peacefully grazing and walked beside the two mounted men.

"You think he's going to show us a Comanche war party?" Tad asked.

"Doubt anything like that. He'd be just as leery of them as anybody else would."

The boy took them nearly a mile from the river. They crossed over the top of a high hill, both Tad and Riot searching the land around them carefully as they walked their horses.

On the far side of the hill they rounded a large rock and came upon three mounds.

"Those Comanches," the boy told them. "Many come. Fight between each other. Those dead. Go away."

"Did those that go away have rifles? Guns?" Riot pointed to the Winchester in his saddle holster.

The boy turned his palms up. "Don't know."

"How long ago? When?"

After much thought, "They go from here, there" — he pointed north — "fourteen days ago."

"Was it Blood Shirt?" Tad asked. "Blood Shirt?"

"Yes!" the boy said emphatically. "Blood Shirt!"

"Well, hell," Riot told Tad, "if they'd got the guns, we'd have sure found out on the way down. Those little villages we passed'd be plowed under."

"Unless they went north by some other route. They know this country as well as I know the Davis Mountains. Probably better."

"We can't give up."

Tad's face was pale. "They may be tearin' the country apart up there right now." A thought came to him. "They'd have buried these braves together with their weapons! Let's look!"

The graves were shallow and poorly filled

in. They scooped out dirt until all three corpses were exposed.

"Not one of them's got a rifle." Riot was thinking out loud. "But they're all dead from rifle slugs. Nothin's proved, one way or the other."

"We gotta hope they didn't get the guns. Maybe couldn't pay for 'em," Tad said. "Maybe that caused the fight. Maybe some of 'em wanted to try to take the guns from the Comancheros by force. Maybe Blood Shirt figured he'd lose too many men, and maybe he's gone back up to try to get more furs or money or whatever the hell he's paying for 'em with."

Riot flipped a dollar to the boy, who had stood by watching with fascination. "Let's quit maybeing, and head for Chihuahua."

The Fourth Month

7

Chihuahua was the biggest town Tad had ever seen. You could ride into it and after a while be completely surrounded by buildings, so that everywhere you looked you were trapped by frame and adobe walls with no sign of the open space around the town. It was unnerving. The streets that wound casually between houses and places of business were jammed with traffic, a profusion of slow-moving carts and wagons and people afoot, mingled with stray dogs, cows that seemed to belong to no one, and chickens pecking in the ground for food.

A big frame building claimed their attention. Its sign read *Hotel de Juárez*, and Riot told Tad, "Soon's we get our horses settled, let's get a couple rooms. We'll maybe be here a while."

The hotel clerk spoke fluent English. After

they'd washed and shaved in their rooms, the two men stopped by at his desk and Riot said, "We're looking for a man. Name of Vinaro."

"Certainly." The man punched a bell and called, "Señor Vinaro!"

An old, bent man with a broom in his hand came into the lobby. *"Qué?"* he muttered.

"This is Señor Vinaro," the clerk said.

Riot lowered an eyebrow in puzzled rejection of Señor Vinaro. "I doubt that's the one we're looking for."

"How many Vinaros are there in Chihuahua?" Tad asked.

The clerk raised his arms wide. "Many, many. I thought you meant our Señor Vinaro." He said to the old man, *"Por nada, Vinaro,"* and waved him back to his work.

"One more thing. Where can we buy some little mirrors, round, about so big." Riot showed the size with his thumb and forefinger. "Painted red on back."

"That would be Cordenas. He paints them red, yellow, all colors on the back. He makes mirrors and fireworks." The clerk walked with them to the door and pointed down the street. "He is down two blocks and left two blocks. There are fiesta firecrackers, pinwheels, things like that in his window."

Walking the last two blocks, they passed a place that was unmistakably a gambling hall. The sounds of chips clicked clearly from within, and there was an occasional clinking of glasses mingled with excited voices. Right next door there was a long, low building with many windows on a level with the dirt street running before it. Girls were leaning out of several of the windows. Some of them chatted back and forth from one window to another. Some of them smiled at the men walking by.

"This's a nice, friendly area," Riot said.

A pretty, slender girl with blue-black hair smiled at them and said softly, *"Bienvenida."*

"No time for that sort of thing," Tad told Riot hastily. His own eyes were still on the girl a few steps later when his foot came down on a chicken lying in the street. The outraged fowl fluttered indignantly and loudly away, and Tad caught himself, made a disgusted sound. "Dumb beast!"

The girl giggled from the window.

Tad turned his eyes to the street before them. "You say anything cute, Riot, and I'll bust you one!"

The second building on the next block, a one-story adobe, was separated from the buildings to each side of it by a few feet. There were two windows, one on each side of the doorway, and they were piled full of dusty fireworks and mirrors of various sizes and shapes. Entering the door, they could hear someone sawing in the back room and they continued on to the back. Tad noticed a mirror on a table, that was identical to the one Colonel Blacker had shown them, and he picked it up to look at it, then followed Riot.

In the back room a bearded, baldheaded man of fifty was sawing through what looked like a round stick. Tad almost dropped the mirror he still held as he realized the round stick was dynamite.

Riot pushed his hat back on his head as the dark-featured man straightened up from his work. "This fellow," he said, "has got the final answer on how to go out with a bang."

The man pointed to a small shelf near him where a religious statue stood next to an open case of dynamite. "Saint Teresa guards me against harm."

"You speak English," said Tad.

"Grew up on the border. Villa Acuña. What can I do for you? I'm Cordenas." The man rubbed his sweating forehead with a hand that had two fingers missing.

"You sell many of these things?" Tad held up the mirror.

Cordenas shrugged. "Not as many as I'd like to. Why?"

"We're hoping maybe we can get a job with the man named Vinaro who's been buying quite a few of those mirrors from you." Riot leaned back against the shelf where the dynamite was and picked up a coil of fuse, dangling it idly in his hand. "We're willing to pay to find out."

Cordenas shook his head. He somehow gave the impression of being on guard and faintly nervous, though his voice was steady. "There are at least twenty Vinaros who buy things from me." He wet his lips. "What kind of work you do?"

Riot tossed the fuse onto the shelf. "Among other things, we've traded with Indians. Especially Comanches."

"Chihuahua ain't Comanche territory. It's Apache."

Riot took two hundred dollars out of his pocket. He held the greenbacks in front of Cordenas. "Can you think of a Vinaro who might need help trading with Comanches along about now?"

The baldheaded man blinked at the money. "No."

"Five hundred?" Riot dug into his pocket again.

"No! Money won't help!" Cordenas picked up his saw. "I have work to do. I'll mention this to my customers named Vinaro. Maybe that will help."

"We're staying at the Hotel de Juárez."

That night they ate in the hotel restaurant and later walked out onto the cool streets of the shadowed town. Riot said, "I hate to tell you this, Tad, but the best place for us to go is that gamblin' district."

"You don't sound too unhappy about it."

"Truth to tell, I ain't." He suddenly caught at Tad's shoulder. Tad's eyes swept the street, his hand going to his gun before he realized that Riot was holding onto him only to keep from falling down.

"What's the matter?" He grabbed Riot's sagging frame and swung the man's back to a wall for additional support.

"Is it your chest?" he demanded, but Riot could not speak. Gritting his teeth against the pain and weakness, it was all Riot could do to breathe.

Tad was sure his friend was dying, but there was nothing he could do but hold him up and wait. After a long time, Riot said, "It's passin'. Be all right."

"Thank God!" Tad whispered.

When Riot was strong enough to stand by himself, Tad said, "Damn, Riot. Damn! Why don't you forget this, and go have yourself some fun before that thing gets to your heart for good! It ain't fair you should spend the little time you got this way!"

Riot stretched his shoulders gently, arching his back. "I'd like to. I'd like a whole lot to forget this, an' you. But I can't do it." He managed to grin. "Besides, just now we're headed for exactly the type place I'd be spendin' my time in anyway. This is no time to try to get rid of me."

At the corner there was a rumble of hoofbeats and a platoon of soldiers rode by. Their uniforms were brilliant blue and red, and the few people in the street scattered to each side to keep from being trampled under the horses' hoofs.

"There goes the law, down here," Riot said. "Heard the army was next to God almighty in Mexico."

They went on to the gambling house. Inside, it was colorless and drab compared to Alpine's Bird Cage, but there was some of the same tension and subdued excitement, the flavor in the air of money to be won. Beyond the gambling tables, at the far side of the room, a bar stretched from wall to wall, and Riot and Tad crossed to it.

On their second drink, a big, hard-faced American with a stubble of beard moved next to them at the bar and ordered tequila. "Hear you boys was lookin' for a man." His voice was deep and gruff. He turned toward them, leaning one elbow on the bar.

"You heard right," Riot said. "Looking for work."

"Don't see too many Americans aroun' here, this far south," the big man continued. "What's your line?"

"Anything they'll pay us for."

"That's bitin' a big chunk."

"Yeah."

"My name's Bud."

Riot waved a thumb at Tad. "He's Tad. I'm Riot."

Bud drank the tequila and put the glass back for another fill. "Live up to the name?"

"Sometimes."

"Let's go to a table an' talk."

Riot bought a bottle and he and Tad followed the other man to a corner table. As they sat down, Riot noticed two heavily armed Mexicans standing by the door and watching them.

Bud saw that Riot had seen them. "They're okay. Friends of mine."

Riot nodded at the bottle he'd put on the table. "Help yourself."

Bud and Riot did most of the drinking and all of the talking. The talk went from the weather and how hot it was to whisky and law. On the law, Bud allowed he hated all lawmen in general and Texas Rangers in particular. Then he said, "Don't your friend here never open his mouth?"

"Doesn't talk much. But speaking of Rangers, up in Presidio he almost killed one with his bare hands a while back."

"How come? What for?"

Tad said, "He asked too many questions."

After about an hour of feeling them out, Bud rubbed his jaw with the back of a hairy hand and leaned forward. "Look, could be my boss'd be willin' to hire you two on for a while. Prob'ly be only for a month, maybe six weeks. Like that. But pay'd be not bad."

"Been wondering when you'd come around to this," Riot said. He made some quick guesses and added, "Cordenas told Vinaro and Vinaro had you come start checking us out."

"You're pretty smart, huh?" The second bottle was about a third empty in front of Bud, and he was feeling it. "But you don't get nothin' out of me."

"I'm not so smart. I'm as dumb as they come. Still can't figure a lot of things. Naturally, I can see that it'll take maybe six weeks more to sell the rifles. And you're goin' to want all the good men on hand you can get, to make sure Blood

Shirt don't take 'em away from you by force. But how is it they weren't sold three weeks ago when Blood Shirt was down here?"

"Three weeks?" Bud grunted. "You *are* pretty dumb. Blood Shirt ain't been south of the river in a year. Them few guns he's got was took to 'im as a come-on."

"No foolin'?" Riot shook his head in mild amazement. "What threw me off, we saw Comanche graves by the Conchos."

"Blood Shirt sent some braves down to try to find the main store of guns. Me an' some fellows shot three or four of 'em."

"Wouldn't it be easier, anyhow, to sell to Apaches, or the Mexican Army?"

"Hah!" Bud took another drink. "Apaches'd be able t'wipe out Chihuahua, and Vinaro along with it, with that much guns and ammunition. Hell, there's even fifteen barrels of black powder in with the deal. An' the Mexican Army'd maybe pay, but they'd turn right around an' steal the money back again. This ain't Comanche country. They ain't in no position t'cheat us. An' they'll be usin' them weapons all up along the border, and through the Texas plains particular."

"Have another drink, Bud."

"Nah." The man got to his feet slowly, and the two armed Mexicans at the door straightened up alertly. "I gotta go back an' tell about the talk we jus' had. I'll be back in 'bout an hour. You wait, huh?"

The big, unshaven man went on a slightly uneven keel to the door and walked out with the two Mexicans following him.

"What do you think?" Tad asked.

"We're almost too lucky to be alive, that's what I'm thinking. Talk about dumb luck!" Riot put his feet on the chair Bud had been sitting in. "We got some time to kill. What about going next door and talking to that little lady who laughed at you when you stepped on the chicken?"

"Nothin' much to talk about. 'Sides, it seems t'me we ought to stick right here until he gets back." Tad's fist was on the table, and he clenched it tight. "I been sittin' here for over an hour fightin' back an urge to shoot him right in the middle of his ugly face."

"I know. I could see it. He seemed to take it as just your natural orneriness." Riot paused. "What about going next door and doing something besides talking to that little lady who laughed at you when you stepped on the chicken?"

"You go ahead. I don't think it'd be right for me."

Riot looked at him closely. "You'd do well to

consider one thing, Tad. There's a fair chance you'll be dead come morning. It'd be a horrible shame to die wanting for a woman. It'd be damned near impossible to do a good job of dying."

"What makes you think I'm in need of a woman?" asked Tad.

"I watched you watching her." Riot stood up. "I also saw another girl in there I believe to be even prettier than she. You comin'?"

8

When they got back to the gambling house, almost an hour had gone by.

They went to the bar. Staring at his drink, not touching it, Tad said, "You know somethin', Riot?"

"What?"

"That . . . it's kinda awkward to put in words. That's the first girl . . ." He let the sentence trail off.

"What? Oh my God, boy, you'll make a philosopher out a me yet." Riot emptied his glass and frowned at it. "I can see right now it ain't how long you live, but what you do with your time that counts."

"That's funny. A preacher once said that, one time when I was in church."

"Probably we don't mean quite the same thing. Main difference being, he was wrong

126

and I'm right."

Riot saw Bud as soon as the man entered the big room. Walking between the tables and gamblers, Bud approached them and said, "Come on. Vinaro wants to talk to you."

The two Mexicans were waiting outside the door, and they fell in behind the three Americans.

"Ain't far," Bud said. "Maybe a fifteen-minute walk."

"What's Vinaro do?" Riot turned toward Bud slightly so that he could see the trailing Mexicans from the corner of his eye.

"You and me'll get along better, the less you're curious." Having said what he thought to be the right thing, Bud added with a shrug, "You name it, he does it. He's the richest man around here."

They came into the secluded, wealthy section of Chihuahua where a few large houses faced each other on tree-lined streets. The biggest, most pretentious house was isolated by a grove of shade trees, with a wide, graveled path for carriages circling around by the front door.

There were several carriages lining the driveway now, and light and the sounds of conversation came from the house.

"He's havin' a li'l party," Bud said. "We'll go in by the side door."

Entering with the two guards still behind them, they came into a deserted corridor and went through the first doorway to their left. Behind them, the guards closed the door. In front of them, a thin middle-aged man sat at a large desk. He was finely dressed in a short black jacket and a sparkling-clean white shirt that showed fine tucks from neck to belt. There was a thin black string tie at his throat, and he had a gray mustache and small, pointed beard. "Your names," he said.

"Riot Holiday. And this is Tad Johnson."

"You've been talking to my man Bud, and you've convinced him you might be of value to me. I'm not convinced."

"No reason you should be, yet," Riot told him, taking a casual step and turning to stand at such an angle that he could see everyone in the room.

"Not long ago, I found that a man I'd just hired was a Texas Ranger. My position is unhappy. I need men. I cannot afford spies. Which are you?"

"They're not Rangers," Bud said. "I can spot one of them from a mile off."

"That's right. We're not." Riot put his hands on his hips so that his right hand was almost touching his gunbutt. "Matter of fact, it's kind of insultin' that you should suggest it."

The two Mexicans behind them swung their guns uncertainly, so that they were almost on a line with Riot. His revolver appeared almost magically in his right hand as his right arm went through an invisibly quick motion. The revolver hammer cocked, was aimed at the two men before they could swing the rifle muzzles to bear on him.

"Put those rifles down."

"They don't speak English," Vinaro said.

"Then you tell them. Or I might have to shoot them."

Vinaro spoke to them in Spanish and they leaned their guns against the wall behind them.

"This is a robbery?" Vinaro asked.

"No." Riot put his gun back. "I just get nervous about having guns pointed at me. If you need help, you better hire us. If not, we'll be leaving."

Vinaro studied Riot, then looked at Tad for a long moment. "All right. You're working for me. Forty a week and keep."

"Who says we'll work for that much?"

"I do. It's good money."

"For riskin' life and limb?"

"When your work is done, I'll give you both another hundred dollars." Vinaro took a long black cigar from a desk drawer and lit it. He got up and walked around the desk. "I know that you know about the guns, and about Blood Shirt. He hasn't got quite enough in money and goods to buy at this time. But he will have. His warriors are currently raiding and looting in Texas, toward that end." Vinaro flicked his cigar ash into a small porcelain tray on his desk. "The trouble with these savages, of course, is that they have no sense of value. They're often so childish that they overlook gold, silver and currency and waste their time collecting worthless scalps."

Tad was across the room in one long lunge. He grabbed Vinaro by the throat and started to choke him as Bud and the two Mexicans grabbed for their guns.

Pivoting swiftly, Riot brought his knee up hard into Bud's groin and the man grunted loudly and doubled up as his half-unholstered revolver flew to the floor. At the same time, Riot's gun was out.

One of the Mexican guards was reaching for a pistol at his belt, and the other was ducking back toward the wall where the rifles were standing. The man going for his pistol seemed to present the more immediate danger, and Riot shot him through the head. The second man had his rifle in his hand when Riot's second bullet caught him in the shoulder. Still alive, and trying to aim the rifle with one good hand, the man turned toward Riot. A third slug slammed him back against the wall.

The door burst open and half a dozen of the brilliantly uniformed soldiers poured into the room. Despite the noise, Riot heard Tad say from slightly behind him now, "I'll kill you, I'll kill you, I swear I'll kill you!"

Riot had time for one more shot that knocked a soldier off his feet, and then the others were swarming against him. He clubbed a squat, greasy-haired soldier over the head, slashed out with his left arm and sent the next man sprawling, before the first had hit the floor.

Two soldiers had Tad by the arms and were dragging him away from Vinaro, who lay still across his desk. Tad suddenly writhed away from them, knocking one of them down.

Three other soldiers were inside the doorway now. Riot fired his last two shots and one of them sagged while the second screamed in pain as he was rocked back through the door by the force of the bullet high in his chest.

Riot and Tad charged across the room now and smashed their way out the door. Armed Mexicans were hurrying in through the door where the two of them had entered before, so they ran down the corridor in the opposite direction. They made a sharp right turn as someone yelled a command in Spanish behind them, and then they charged into a large room where at least fifty men and women were gathered.

The women were dressed formally. Almost all of the men were young and in uniform. As Riot and Tad rushed into sight the women shrieked almost in chorus and retreated toward the far side of the elegant room.

Riot, still on a dead run, simply raised an elbow to knock the first soldier out of his way. He hesitated, to decide which way to go, and another army man jumped him from the side. It took him an instant to shake the man off, and then they were at him from all sides.

Tad jumped forward and turned so that his back rested solidly on Riot's back, and they started making progress through their dense crowd of enemies. Walking backwards, keeping the feel of Riot's body against his own, Tad swung both fists furiously. He was hit several times, and was partially aware of the fact that a sabre slashed him shallowly across the chest, but the faces that appeared around him became bloody or disappeared.

Leading, Riot battered his way through the sea of faces, arms and fists. Two men before him and to his right tripped backwards over a long, beautifully set table. He worked toward the table, grabbed the end of it and heaved, his surging strength lifting it and tossing it into the crowd before him. He saw the door and he cleared the way of at least two men with a right and a left, and then something struck him with blinding force in the chest.

When Riot went down, Tad was stopped, his arms pinned to his sides, almost immediately.

Riot's head cleared quickly, even though his chest was throbbing with pain. He was sitting in a chair with his hands tied at his back. Near him, in another chair, Tad was bound and was watching the people around him. They were still in the large room, and the table Riot had thrown was still on its side. Men and women were talking in loud, excited voices in Spanish.

Seeing that Riot was awake, Tad said, "I'm sorry I went after him."

"Did you kill him?"

"I don't know."

At that moment Vinaro walked through the door. He spoke in a calm, unhurried voice to the others and they became quiet. Then he walked to the two tied men and said, "I've explained that you thieves tried to rob me." He turned to a swarthy, thick-set officer with a flattened, shapeless nose, who stood beside him. "Colonel Ruiz is taking you prisoner. The army has a splendid jail for thieves and murderers such as yourselves."

Colonel Ruiz said in labored English, "Is too bad for you Señor Vinaro gives the party tonight for me and my officers." He gave gruff orders in Spanish and four soldiers pushed Riot and Tad to their feet and took them out of the house.

The soldiers waited while one of Vinaro's servants brought a wagon around to the front of the house. Then they hoisted the two men up and dropped them into the back of the wagon.

As the wagon bumped along over the road, Tad said, "God, I'm sorry, Riot. It was a loco thing I did. But when he sat there flickin' his ashes and talking about scalps, I thought of Ma and the kid brother, Tom."

"You did what seemed right to you just then. Only mistake you made was not to shoot him. Choking takes time."

One of the soldiers said angrily, *"Silencio!"*

"Guess he wants us to be quiet." Riot looked up at the soldier's shadowy figure and said, "Your mother is a pig."

"Silencio!" The man leaned down in the wagon and struck Riot in the face with his fist.

Riot strained his eyes in the dark to see the man's face. The moon came from behind a cloud, and he saw a square, brutal face with a white scar over the left eye.

"I will remember you, son of a pig," Riot said clearly.

The soldier cursed, leaned down and hit Riot once more, then kicked him in the side.

The fortress was at the far side of Chihuahua, on the outskirts of the town. It looked like a large, gray box of stone, and there were guards patrolling the thirty-foot-high walls.

One of the soldiers shouted before the thick oak gate, and after a few seconds it swung open and the wagon was driven through it.

The soldiers talked to an officer who seemed to be in charge, and Riot and Tad were dragged to their feet in the wagon, then pushed onto the ground below.

Riot noticed that the prison took in a comparatively small part of the army compound, and that it was in a corner so that two of its walls were actually the stones that made up that corner of the main wall.

They were taken to the jailhouse. The officer unlocked the large door to the jail. Inside, there were six cells to each side of a long corridor. One of the cells was unlocked and the soldier with the scar over his eye pushed them inside, shoving hard and fast so that they stumbled in the dark and fell to the stone floor.

When they were alone in the pitch-black cell,

Tad at last said, "Do you think they'll kill us in the morning?"

"I hope not."

"I been thinkin' about a thing. What you said about girls. I'm glad I went to see that girl who laughed when I stepped on the chicken. I didn't understand a word she said to me. But it didn't matter. She was a sweet little girl, with an exciting sort of kindness in her eyes. And a man who died not having had a woman wouldn't really have lived."

9

By the morning light that came in through the small, single window placed high in the cell, they could see that there was one cot in the barren room – nothing more.

Before the sun was up, the main prison door was opened and haggard prisoners from the other cells were released. Soon the sound of hammers pounding against stone could be heard from outside.

It was midmorning when the main door was opened once more, and Vinaro and Colonel Ruiz, with two armed guards at their sides, came down the corridor. One of the guards unlocked the cell and checked to see that they were still tied. Then Vinaro and Ruiz came in.

"Three men were killed last night, and eight will be no good for some time," Vinaro said. He was wearing a high collar that didn't quite hide the black bruises on his throat. "Your two lives are a poor price to pay for the damage to my home alone."

"Leave them to me," Ruiz said. "I will make them suffer a great much until they die."

Vinaro shook his head. "I do not want them to die yet. I will be too busy for some time to deal with them in the leisurely fashion I have in mind. I will leave them in your care until later, Colonel. A few weeks on your rock pile will give them time to think about what I have in store for them."

"Ruiz," Tad said, "do you know Vinaro's selling nearly a thousand rifles to the Comanches? Couldn't the army use those guns?"

"I am not the army. I am a simple colonel, and Señor Vinaro is a friend of mine. His business transactions, they are no concern of mine."

Vinaro spoke to Ruiz in Spanish and left the jail. When he was gone, the colonel spoke to the two guards, who went to Riot and Tad and began going carefully through their pockets.

They took everything they found on the two men, even their spurs and jackets and hats, and the man who searched Riot murmured with surprise at finding nearly five hundred dollars in one pants pocket. He grunted again as he took Riot's wallet from the jacket and glanced at the money inside it.

"All you want's the money," Riot said. "I'd like the wallet back."

"Why?" Ruiz took it from the man and glanced quickly through the leather compartments. "More than a thousand dollars. But you care more about the wallet? Ah! Could this be why?" A broad smile spread under his flat nose as he pulled a pressed, still-yellow marigold from the billfold. "The thief and murderer is sentimental, eh?" He put the flower back, and stuck the wallet in a jacket pocket.

Riot said once more, "I want the wallet."

"If you really want the flower back, come to my safe and get it." Ruiz turned and walked away. The guards untied the two men and followed him, locking the doors behind them.

Tad looked at Riot strangely. "That was the marigold Roslyn gave you. You been carryin' it all this time."

Rubbing his wrists to get circulation back, Riot said, "Let's take a look at that cut you got across your chest."

"It's nothin' much. That was Roslyn's flower."

"What about it?"

"You like her?"

"Course I do."

"I mean, you like her a lot? Not like a sister, I mean, like a girl?"

Riot sat on the single cot. He glanced briefly at Tad and said, "Yes."

"Well, why'n hell didn't you never let on, for hell's sake?" Tad said angrily. "She was cryin' more for you than for me when we took off!"

"You're crazy." Riot stood and looked up at the window and the sky beyond. "And you're forgetting that I haven't much time left."

The next morning they were taken out with the other twenty or so prisoners and fed a poisonous-tasting soup for breakfast. They ate in the yard outside the jail and then walked a few yards to where heavy sledge hammers were leaning against the fort wall. There was a pile of boulders nearby, and the prisoners went to work breaking them up. Guards armed with whips and revolvers were in the compound beside them, and other soldiers with rifles strolled along the wall above.

By noon one of the men working near them stumbled under the weight of the hammer in his hands and fell down. A whiplash whistled through the air and cracked savagely over his back. The guard yelled, *"Arriba! Arriba!"* and struck him again. The man struggled slowly to his feet and went to work once more in the now blazing sun. Later in the afternoon, his hands began to shake as though he were bitterly cold, and he fell again. The jailers lashed him brutally, and when he did not move, they threw water on him. At last they realized that he was dead, and two of them dragged him away by his feet.

That night, lying in the dark of their cell, Riot said, "Well, guess it's time for us to start getting out of here."

"We bang our heads through the wall?"

"Nope. We dig out. Only way I can see."

"With what? They don't even give you spoons to eat the soup with, and they took our knives, even our spurs. You got strong fingernails?"

"What I've got isn't much better. That stuff we been breaking up is granite. I got a couple of good-sized, sharp pieces of it in my pocket."

They moved the cot away from the wall between them and freedom and started scraping against the concrete where marks would not show when the bed was moved back in place. Within a few minutes their hands and fingers were numb and badly skinned. "Can't let our fingers get all bloody," Riot said, feeling his wet hand in the dark. "Might get 'em curious." He ripped off part of his shirttail and wrapped part of the cloth around his own hand and gave the other part to Tad.

"This'll work sure as hell," Tad said. "But it

might take twenty years."

"You know any better way?"

"No."

"Then go to it."

Two days later they had to steal new chips of granite from the stone pile, for the original pieces had worn down to slivers too small to hold. The jail wall was marked so little it was doubtful whether a guard would have noticed their efforts if he'd looked behind the cot.

They could not work all day and all night too, and so they began to sleep half a night each, judging time as best they could. The rock dust they gathered, pitifully small piles at first, was thrown out the window before daylight.

After two weeks of grueling work both in and out of the cell, there was a rounded hole in the wall no more than an inch deep. Then one night Riot woke Tad up and whispered with an edge of deep excitement, "It's gettin' softer! The edge of my cutting stone just went in maybe an eighth of an inch!"

"I'll be damned!" Tad tried cutting into the wall, with the same result. "It's a cheap job of buildin'! We oughtta go in fine style now!"

"No matter how this job goes, this just ain't my style," Riot murmured as he worked. "But it sure beats twiddlin' your thumbs."

There were occasional, unexpected checks at night, but the large outer door made enough noise and took enough time to open, to allow them to cover up their work. The inside of the wall, as they went deeper, sometimes crumbled beneath their hands, and disposing of the dust and tiny pieces of rock became a major problem. They made small holes in their pockets, and walked into the compound in the morning with their hands in the pockets full of dust. Then they emptied their hands and removed them from the pockets, and the dust slowly sifted through the holes and down onto the prison yard.

They began to pry loose rocks as big as a man's head, and these they left in the wall, at night removing them to continue their work. The cloth they used to protect their hands wore out, and they chanced staging a brief fight together in the prison yard so that Tad could tear Riot's shirt half off, and avert suspicion of the ragged shirt.

Tad was weakening, and Riot began doing most of the patient, hellishly hard scratching and digging. It was particularly punishing on his chest, lying with both hands stretched before him into the wall, and twice the muscles in his chest rebelled as they had before, and the fiery hot pain made him lose consciousness briefly both times.

Nearly four weeks after they'd been put in the cell, Riot was working long before dawn, most of the top half of his body in the hole. He was working by feel, cutting fiercely at a fist-sized rock he was trying to dislodge, when the rock suddenly slipped from touch and he heard a faint sound of falling stone before him. Pushing backwards and twisting to get out, he said, "Tad! We're through!"

Tad scrambled from the bed and squeezed into the hole. When he backed out, he grabbed Riot's forearm in a hard, happy grip. "We figured another foot or two! We might get outa here tonight!"

"With luck."

An hour later, straining through the tight hole, Riot squeezed out the far side. To his surprise, he was about six feet up from the ground that lay in dark shadows beneath him. There was nothing else to do but dive head first to the ground and break his fall with his hands. He did, dropping almost soundlessly to the earth. Lying still for a moment, he listened to the silence around him, then got to his feet.

"Come on," he whispered into the dark hole, noticing that they had been digging into a part of the fort where the wall had decayed away, leaving the wall thinner there.

Tad got one hand out. The other appeared, and he started to pull himself, inching through. Riot could now see Tad's face by the moonlight. Suddenly, Tad stopped moving. "Riot," he said in a faint, thin voice, "I can't get all the way out."

"Come on. You're my size!"

"I can't do it!" He grunted with the effort he was making. "I must be thicker!"

"The hell you are!" A sudden thought gripped Riot and he said tensely, "Get back! Get back in a hurry!" He put his hand up to give Tad something to shove against and the dark hole was soon empty. Riot put his hand into the opening and felt the rocks above. Then he whispered to Tad, "Think the goddam rocks in it are easin' down. You better not try to come through again. Might be a lot of weight about to bust loose there."

"I gotta try!"

"No. I'll be back pretty quick."

Riot moved away from the wall. Looking back, he saw a guard walk into sight on top of the wall, and he ducked to the side of a giant saguaro cactus a few feet before him. Then the guard walked on, and Riot ran through the night toward the dim, outlying houses of Chihuahua.

Not far from the houses, he saw a solitary soldier riding toward the fort. Slowing to an easy walk, Riot headed for the man, beginning to whistle a low, tuneless song as he approached.

The soldier reined his horse toward Riot and said a few words in an arrogant voice. By the time he suspected something was wrong, it was too late.

Riot rushed the startled animal and grabbed the reins just behind the jaw. The horse's instinctive action was to try to rear away, and Riot encouraged this by pulling the bit back hard in the animal's mouth. The horse reared high into the air and Riot let the reins run through his fingers. The soldier, trying to hold on, was jerked from the saddle to the ground as Riot caught him by the jacket and pulled.

Without letting go of the horse, Riot stepped toward the soldier as the man sprang to his knees, grabbing for the revolver at his side. Riot's booted foot caught the soldier on the face so hard that it flipped him over onto his back. Hauling the still frightened horse after him, Riot bent down and took the gun from the prone man's holster. Then, as he started to move feebly, Riot slammed the revolver barrel against his head, and he lay still.

Shoving the revolver into his belt, Riot swung onto the horse and galloped into the dark streets of Chihuahua.

At this hour the streets were almost completely deserted, and Riot didn't break his gallop until he brought the horse to a quick stop in front of Cordenas's darkened shop. Hitching the reins to a post, Riot took the gun from his belt and went to the door. It was locked, and he kicked it in with his boot.

A lamp sputtered to life in the back room as Riot walked toward it. Cordenas was standing there in his underwear, a rifle leveled toward Riot as he entered the doorway.

Riot looked at the rifle and then at Cordenas. He waved the revolver in his hand and said, "Put it down. Or do I have to kill you?"

The Mexican stood his ground. "We will both be killed if you don't leave."

"You're at a terrible disadvantage." Riot grinned. "I don't give a damn about dying. How do you feel?"

The Mexican stared at Riot and knew he was telling the truth. His shoulders sagged, and he lowered the rifle. "What do you want?"

Riot took the man's gun away and returned his revolver to his belt. "I'm going to rob you."

"I'm a poor craftsman trying to make a living!" Cordenas protested.

Riot started searching the back room. "I believe that. That's why I'm not going to kill you." There were two or three gunny sacks on the floor. Riot picked one up and emptied a half-full box of dynamite on the shelf into the sack.

Cordenas went white. "Be careful, hombre!" he whispered.

"You were sawin' the stuff. It ain't that delicate."

"Saw, you can do. Slow, not much heat. But bang it around, no!"

"How do you set this stuff off? I want to blow up the jail."

"You can't without dynamite caps. A little explosion to make a big explosion. You stick them in the end of the dynamite."

Riot rubbed his jaw, staring at the floor. "Will firecrackers work?"

Cordenas's face took on a look of professional interest. "I don't know. I never thought of it. Maybe."

"If you hear a big bang, you'll know. Where are some firecrackers? And some matches and a fuse?" Riot pulled his gun again. "Don't say you ain't got any."

"I'll help you if you'll try to release Manuel Cordenas, my uncle."

"Done."

"You'll have to hurry. There'll be daylight in an hour or two." Cordenas pointed to a thick canvas sack on the shelf. "Take that. There are plenty of firecrackers in there. I was making them for the Fiesta of St. Matthew." He opened a drawer in the table and took out a thick loop of fuse. "Here. And matches." He threw a box of matches into the gunny sack as Riot added the canvas bag. "That fuse is for firecrackers, too. You couldn't set off firecrackers very well with dynamite fuse, and I haven't got any left anyway."

Riot picked up the twenty-pound sack and started for the door.

"Remember one thing!" Cordenas called. "That fuse will burn ten times as fast as dynamite fuse!"

Riot galloped to the edge of town, within sight of the fort. The moon went behind a cloud as he rode across the flats with the sack in his hand, and glancing at the cloud, he judged he'd have ten minutes of almost total darkness.

He slowed the horse to a walk as he came within hearing of the fort, then he tied it at a distance, took the rifle from its saddle, and approached the wall quietly.

Tad was waiting on his side of the hole, and Riot whispered, "Pick up the cot and get behind it in the corner. I'm goin' to dynamite this hole." He passed the rifle to Tad.

"You know how to use that stuff?" He pulled the gun through.

"I'm inventing my own way as I go along. Get back and hold your ears."

Tad picked up the cot with its straw-stuffed mattress and stood behind it in the farthest corner of the cell. "Try not to blow me up, too," he whispered loudly.

Reaching into the sack, Riot took out six sticks of dynamite, bit at his lower lip speculatively, and put back two of them. He took a large firecracker from the smaller canvas bag inside the gunny sack. It had a fuse on it about three inches long.

Riot put the four sticks side by side in his hand. Looks about right to widen the hole some, he thought. He put three sticks in the hole, and forced his thumb into one end of the fourth stick until the end was crushed back under the pressure. Then he jammed the firecracker into the broken end as far as he could. He stuck the stick of dynamite between his teeth and felt through the gunny sack with both hands until he found the box of matches. He removed a handful and stuck them in his pocket, except for one.

Placing the last stick with the other three, Riot picked up the gunny sack with his left hand. With his right, he struck the match. He held the flame to the end of the firecracker fuse until it caught and fizzed with sparks, and then he started to run. He'd gone about five long steps when the world exploded in a gigantic roar that he felt more than heard.

Riot went flying with the gunny sack still clutched in his hand. He hit the ground and rolled over twice as pieces of rock whizzed by him. When he looked back at the wall, there was a gaping black hole nearly six feet high, and enough rubble was piled at the foot of the wall for him to climb easily up into the cell on its higher level.

As Riot got into the cell, Tad tossed away the splintered bed and said, "Jesus! You damn near knocked down the whole wall!"

Going to the door, Riot shot the lock off with his revolver, then kicked it open. Guards on the wall above could now be heard yelling and shooting aimlessly in the dark. "They'll expect us to go running out that hole. We'll fool 'em and bust up the rest of the fort. Go out and see if you can shoot the locks off the other cells."

As Tad went into the corridor, Riot knelt in the dark and started pushing open the ends of more sticks of dynamite and inserting firecrackers into them. In the second cell Tad opened, the prisoners had somehow smuggled a sledge hammer into the jail and stuffed it into their straw mattress. One of them carried it out and started smashing the iron locks on the other doors.

When Tad got back to Riot, eight sticks were capped. Riot stuck them in his pockets. "Here." He thrust the gunny sack toward Tad. "You can shoot with one hand better than I can light an' throw dynamite with one hand. Follow me. An' don't bump that sack around."

Tad put two shots through the lock on the main door and three Mexican prisoners forced it open. The firepower from the walls was being drawn to two of the prisoners who had dashed out through the hole in the wall of the Americans' cell.

As the main body of prisoners surged out of the door into the compound a shout went up from the wall and the guards gathered there turned their fire on them.

Holding the rifle with one hand, Tad shot one of the guards as a prisoner near him was hit and went down. Riot flicked his thumb over a match in his left hand and held it to the short fuse protruding from the stick of dynamite in his right hand. As the fuse caught, he drew his hand back and threw the dynamite high into the air. It could be seen sparking faintly as it arched down toward the top of the wall. Then it exploded with a blasting bang, and the guards gathered there stopped shooting.

Some Mexican prisoners were now rushing the fortress gate and others scattered through the compound as the rest of the army began coming to life in the barracks.

Riot called, "This way, Tad!" He ran past the corner of the jail and crossed a wide stretch of ground that brought him to the officers' quarters. Colonel Ruiz occupied the top floor of the building, and there were wooden stairs leading up to his rooms. Tad, the sack over his shoulder and the rifle in his right hand, pounded up the steps behind Riot.

A group of soldiers rushed out of the barracks closest to the officers' quarters and saw the two men nearly at the top of the stairs.

As bullets screamed and splintered through the wooden steps, Riot struck another match, and an instant later what looked to the soldiers below like a giant, spitting firecracker sailed away from the stairs toward them. The explosion rocked the stairs.

"Come on!" Riot said.

Ruiz was pulling on his boots as the two men pushed open his bedroom door. The colonel reached for a revolver hanging from his bedpost and Tad shot him, aiming the rifle from his hip.

As Tad cradled the rifle under his right arm and tossed the bolt back and forward with a twist of his wrist, Riot bent over the colonel. The officer was dying, but his eyes were open. "I came to get my wallet," he said. "Where's the safe and how do I get into it?"

"Go hell," Ruiz muttered.

Riot took a stick of explosive from his pocket and held it above the man's face. "Maybe you been wonderin' what was making all the racket. This is the stuff." He lit a match and held the flame close to the fuse with a steady hand. "Tad," he called, "get out of the room!" He turned back to Ruiz. "I'd just as soon touch it off." He moved the match flame closer to the fuse.

Ruiz stared in horror at the dynamite a few inches from his face. It was so close that he went slightly crosseyed watching it and his mouth trembled. "You're crazy!"

"Matter of principle. Match is gettin' low, and I ain't going to light another."

"All right! Safe's in the office. Key's in the desk there." The colonel's gaze went to a small desk in the bedroom.

Riot blew out the match and put the dynamite back in his pocket.

The safe contained his wallet, and the marigold was still in it. So was the money. There were two Colt revolvers with full cartridge belts hanging from the wall near the safe. Riot took

154

them both, and as he was leaving the room, he noticed his and Tad's hats sitting on top of a filing cabinet in the corner. In the next room, where Tad was watching the fortress yard from a window, Riot said, "Have a sidegun and a hat."

Tad pulled the hat on and started buckling the belt around his waist. "They're startin' to get some order down there," he said, still watching through the glass. "That was quite a bluff you pulled on Ruiz, tellin' me to leave the room, an' all," he added.

Riot didn't answer, and Tad glanced at him, suddenly wondering if it had been a bluff. "You wouldn't've been that loco?"

There were footsteps on the stairs and Riot said, "Can't use dynamite on them. We'd knock out our own way of getting down. Open that door soon's I light a stick." He touched a match flame to one of the sticks, and Tad slammed the door open.

Riot tossed the explosive out and a moment later there was a roar from below. He went out the door while the noise was still punishing his ears, and started shooting into the men coming up the stairs. There were four of them. One of them was the man with the scar over his eye, and Riot made a point of shooting him first. Riot was three steps down on his third shot, and the men before him, though only two of them had been hit, were rolling back down the stairs under the pounding force of his bullets. Tad was now jumping down the steps behind him.

The scar-faced man, blood trailing from both corners of his lips, grasped the railing of the stairs and managed to hold on for a moment. Riot reached him and knocked him over the railing with the back of his left fist. As he pitched over the side, Riot called, *"Silencio,* yourself!" and then he ran down the rest of the steps and raced back toward the jail.

The two men were halfway between the officers' quarters and the jail when a squad of soldiers rushed toward them from the gate. The squad halted to fire and a bullet ruffled Riot's already torn shirt. He stopped to light a match, and in his hurry lit the fuse nearly a third of the way from the tip. As a soldier yelled, *"Cuidado!"* he threw hard and fast, but the dynamite still went off soon enough to knock him and Tad down.

Then they were up and on their feet again, running toward the jail.

"Aren't you gettin' kinda careless with that stuff?" Tad panted.

They ran down the jail corridor and through their old cell, and jumped down to the earth below. "Chances are we maybe got a horse left around here," Riot said.

The soldier's horse had pulled out the chunk of sagebrush Riot had tied him to, but the chunk had caught in some other sage farther away, and the animal was standing with wide, frightened eyes rolling in the moonlight.

Riot jerked the reins free and swung to saddle. He took the sack from Tad and took his foot out of the left stirrup. Tad stepped up behind him. The overloaded pony staggered into a run across the flats.

"We goin' to Vinaro's place?" Tad asked.

"Yeah."

Tad swore as they rode the horse into the rich section of town. There were lights in most of the homes in Chihuahua, as citizens woke up and wondered what was going on at the fort. But the Vinaro home was completely dark. "Looks as if he ain't there!"

Inside the house they found three servants cowering in a room off the kitchen. Otherwise, the place was empty. Riot said, "You want to check the stables out back, Tad? I'll see if I can get anything out of these people."

He lit a candle and studied the servants. Two of them were old women, and a third was an ancient man who was shaking with fear. "Vinaro!"

Riot said. "Where's Vinaro?"

They each shook their heads in turn as he looked from one to another of them. Taking a deep breath, Riot walked over to the old man. He raised his gun, and hoping one of the women would talk, said, "I'll break your head if I have to, to find out."

But it was the old man who blurted out, "Señor Vinaro . . ." He gulped for breath and spoke in rapidfire Spanish, but Riot made out "Señor Vinaro" and "Rio Conchos."

Tad came in. "Vinaro's a horse thief, too. I found our ponies out there, and our gear in a big closet, all tore up from bein' looked through."

They herded the three old people out of the house and into the long, low stables. They got their gear together and saddled their horses. Leaving the three servants locked in the big closet, they rode out into the night that would soon turn to day. As they went by the house, Riot said, "I'd like to leave a calling card." He removed the gunny sack he'd tied to the pommel of his saddle and went into the house.

A few minutes later he hurried out and leaped into the saddle, his dynamite sack still in his hand. They rode away from the house.

The explosion was disappointing. The thick adobe of the big house absorbed much of the sound, and nothing spectacular happened. The roof simply fell in and the windows shattered. And then one wall leaned in slowly and fell on top of the roof.

They rode quickly around the far edge of the town, away from the fort, and by the first light of dawn they were in the foothills to the east. Looking back from the top of a rise, they could see signs of frantic excitement in the town, and riders were dashing back and forth between the houses and the fort.

Riot tenderly patted the sack hanging from his pommel. "That dynamite is purely great stuff. It sure gives people somethin' to talk about."

AUGUST

The Fifth Month

10

During the first days of their ride to the Rio Conchos, they slept by day and rode by night, keeping to the hardest, most rocky land they could find. Much of the barren, desolate country offered little more hiding place than the low, stiff-branched greasewood that covered the land, but there were occasional hills and gullies where they could lay up during the day without being seen. Four times they saw Mexican soldiers patrolling the country for them, and then, as they moved further from Chihuahua, the soldiers appeared no more.

When they at last came to the wide, rolling river, it was early morning, and the rising sun to the east glinted golden on the brown surface of the water.

"This's gonna be a needle in a haystack," Tad

said, studying the low hills to each side of the river. "If the guns're along the Conchos, an' if the sale ain't been completed yet, the rifles could be stored as much as five miles to either side of the river."

"Yeah. In a cave, a house, a hole in the ground." Riot shrugged. "All we can do is look. Work up the river. Keep high as we can on each side, so's we can see as far as possible. Vinaro must have a good crowd with him. And Blood Shirt might have half the Comanche nation by now. If they're to be seen, we ought to see them."

"Let's get on with it."

"You swim?"

Tad shook his head. "Never learned."

"Well, here." Riot took the gunny sack with the dynamite and firecrackers off his saddle and handed it to Tad. "I can swim some, so I'll go to the other side."

Riot went on down to the river. His pinto balked when he got knee-deep into the water, and planted all four feet at a stubborn angle. Riot got off and tugged at the reins, coaxing him gently, not wanting to spook the animal of water if they were to be crossing it from time to time, and finally the gelding stuck his nose in the air, jumped into the deeper water and struggled across the Conchos with Riot

161

swimming beside him.

The first four days on the river, they saw nothing, not a sign of a living person having ever been along the Conchos since the beginning of time. On the fifth day, in more rugged country, where steep, rocky cliffs sometimes fell straight down to the riverbed, Riot looked across the river and saw a cave at the edge of the water. Tad would not be able to see it since it was almost directly below him.

Riding his pinto down an incline to the river, Riot swam across with his horse. Tad saw them coming and rode down a rocky slope to meet them.

Tying his gelding to a fallen log at the river's edge, Riot said, "Cave back here a ways."

They walked upriver about fifty yards. Even before the cave itself came into view, they could see where faint, jagged lines had been made in the rock outside the cave floor.

"What in hell?" Tad said.

Inside the deep, shallow cave Riot struck a match. By its flickering glare, several deep, straight indentations in the earth could be seen. Farther toward the back, there were round cuts in the soft ground. Tad leaned down and picked up a small shred of canvas near one of the numerous footprints on the cave floor. "What you make of it?"

"The rifles were here. The barrels of gunpowder. And I'd say probably a good-sized raft, too. Nails on the bottom of it would explain those marks in the rocks, dragging it out to the river."

"He's a shrewd fellow, Vinaro," said Tad. "Can move the stuff around on a raft, hide it plenty of places along the river, and do his bargainin' from the middle of a wide stretch of water."

Several days later, near nightfall, Riot was on his side of the Conchos when he heard the sound of many hoofbeats. Here the river ran through steeply rolling country, and he estimated the approaching horses were behind a hill two or three hundred yards from the river. He dismounted and pulled the pinto behind a sharp-falling bank of dirt that sloped on down to the water some distance behind him. Glancing across the river, he realized that Tad must have seen his maneuver and was now hidden from sight.

Taking his Winchester from the saddle, he dug his toes into the dirt bank and climbed up a few feet to where he could watch the land beyond.

The hoofbeats became louder, and a band of Comanches swung into view around the hill.

Riding at a lope, they were visible for perhaps two minutes, and then they were gone.

Riot gave them plenty of time to get well out of hearing, then rode the paint down to the river and crossed over. Tad, leading his black, met him at the water's edge. "What was it?"

"Comanches. Ten or fifteen of 'em. Hunting party, I'd guess. Yet they didn't have game and weren't looking for it. Making too much noise. They seemed to be in a hurry to get somewhere — back to camp most likely."

"Comanche hunters without game ain't in a hurry to get home, 'less there's a party or some such comin' up." He got on his black. "You better stick on this side, them bein' on the far side."

Riot turned to his horse as the pinto swung its tail at a fly on its rump, and the thick wand of horse hair brushed his chest. He stopped, puzzled, and glanced down at himself. Then, not speaking, he swung up to the paint.

"What's the matter?" Tad asked.

"Nothing."

"Yeah?" Tad pulled his black over to a point near Riot and pulled back the torn, open shirt. "God damn," he said. "You're infected!" A stretch of skin the size of a hand was red and sore-looking, low on Riot's chest beneath the arrow wound. Tad dropped the shirt back over the inflamed place. "Must be painful t'make you feel a tail slap like that." He sighed deep. "Rotten damn luck!"

Riot said, "We can't slow down just because I'm fallin' apart. Let's go!"

They rode on, moving fast but cautiously now, and in less than a mile's ride they saw the big encampment. Riot was in the lead, and near the top of a small, steep hill by a bend in the wide river, when he suddenly dropped from his horse and pulled the animal back with his hand on its nostrils. "They're across the river there."

"How many?"

"Roughly ten million."

11

Tying their horses at the bottom of the hill, they ran back up the short distance to the top and stretched out to study the Comanche encampment. Only a few tepees were standing in the wide flat across the river. There was no excess equipment; not a woman or child was in the camp; there was nothing to slow them down.

Tad whispered in awe. "There must be three hundred of 'em! An' every man a prime warrior."

Halfway out in the Conchos, where it was wide and deep by the riverbend, there was a large raft piled with crates and barrels. There were about fifteen men at one end of the raft, Mexicans and Americans, bristling with guns. Tad squinted in the fading light and said, "Big fellow on the raft — Ain't that Bud?"

"Uh-huh." Riot glanced away from the raft, his eyes scanning the camp. On the far bank, some distance down the river, there was a small mountain of furs. Trade goods. Part of the price of the rifles. On the near bank, lined up as close as possible to the raft, there were about fifty horses and some light wagons. Vinaro was ready to get away fast, once the trade was made. There were only three or four men standing guard over the Mexican's horses and wagons.

The Comanches were gathering in a huge mob around the few tents now, and some of the Indians were piling wood for large feast fires. "They probably been here quite a while," Riot guessed. "Things're reaching a high point."

"Think they'll trade tonight?"

"Looks that way."

The large fires in the distant Comanche camp were lighted now, and the biggest of the tepees had been opened from the inside. Blood Shirt appeared, and behind him Vinaro and an American in rough, black clothes.

Riot counted seven Mexicans and four Americans grouping around Vinaro as Blood Shirt stepped close to the council fire outside his tent. A drum beat started as a witch doctor dressed in a buffalo robe and horns, his face painted grotesquely, began to dance in jerking motions around the fire while he shook a rattle frantically in each hand.

As darkness became complete, one of the Mexicans near Vinaro handed him a rifle, and Vinaro gave it in turn to Blood Shirt. The shaman finished his dance, and the drum slowed to a stop. A warrior shot an arrow straight into the sky.

Blood Shirt raised the rifle in his hands and fired rapidly into the sky, his left hand working swiftly with the lever-action gun. He shot eight times, and the gun was empty.

And then the falling arrow came down near the fire.

A thunderous roar of approval went up from the Comanche warriors.

"It sure as hell looks like the deal's goin' through right now," Tad said. He squinted at the raft once more, which was dimly visible in the leaping lights thrown by the burning fires in the Comanche camp. "There's enough stuff piled on that raft to start a good-sized war!"

"Uh-huh." Riot moved back away from the top of the hill toward the horses. "Let's get busy."

They hurried quietly down to the animals, and Riot took the gunny sack from his saddlehorn and spoke in a low voice as he worked. "Hobble the horses an' toss 'em on their sides soon's I'm gone. If I can swim out there and set that powder off, it'll likely stampede every standin' horse within five miles." He took the last five sticks of dynamite from the sack, then grabbed the bottom of his shirt and ripped a long, narrow strip from it to tie the sticks together. "You know," he grunted, "I never realized how handy a thing a shirt can be."

"You gonna swim out?"

"Yeah." Riot punched a hole in the end of the center stick and started searching through the gunny sack for a firecracker. There were no loose ones, so he opened the large thick canvas bag inside the gunny sack and scooped a few off the top. "You got a better idea?"

Tad hesitated for a long moment. "No. I guess not. But I can't swim."

"Believe me, if you could swim I'd let you make the trip. I'm getting sick of that muddy water." Riot tied a four-foot length of firecracker fuse onto the three-inch fuse of one of the crackers. "This'll give me some time to swim off."

"How 'bout both of us shooting rifle slugs into the barrels?" Tad knelt down beside Riot. "How 'bout it? That oughtta set it off!"

Riot shook his head. "Chancy. Maybe it'd work, maybe not. Don't know."

"Maybe you'll make it to that raft and maybe not!"

"Anyway, shootin' would give us away, show 'em where we are. We wouldn't last long enough to try somethin' else, if a slug didn't set the powder off." Riot stuck several matches under the cloth wrapped around the dynamite. He took off his gun, hat and boots. "They're far enough downriver so that it'll take me some time to get 'em. Take care of these things for me. If I don't make it, then you can start shooting at the powder. If I do make it, you'll probably be the only man around here with a horse or two to call his own. Try to get down the river. That's where I'll be. And if you don't find me, don't wait."

Riot turned and moved silently toward the river. As he stepped into the shallow water, he heard the heavy thud of a horse falling to the ground behind him. He was wading out to where the Conchos was deeper when now more dimly, he heard a second horse go down.

Water was almost to his throat when an idea came to him. He circled back toward the shore until he saw a floating tree branch caught behind a rock in a small eddy of the river. He pulled the branch out into the river and shoved off into the deeper water, pushing it before him. In mid-stream, he let it float with the slow current, keeping his head and the hand holding the dynamite hidden by the network of twigs and leaves.

He came to a bend in the river where he could see the Comanche camp. The river was now lighted with torches. The trade had begun, and half a dozen large, flaming brands had been set up at the Comanche edge of the Conchos. The ammunition raft had not been moved, but two Mexican boatmen were poling a small boat loaded with furs across to the other side. The boatmen passed within fifty yards of the slowly floating branch as they moved quickly through the water to the Mexican side. There, other men grabbed the bales of furs and tossed them into waiting wagons, and the boatmen started back. This time, the floating branch and the small boat were going to pass close to each other. Riot considered holding the branch, keeping it from moving at the speed of the current, but decided to keep moving as before.

In the dim yellow light and the dark brown shadows caused by the torches and their reflections on the water, Riot saw the boat come closer and closer. They were going to pass within a few yards of each other. He could see one of the boatmen clearly, a heavily mustached Mexican with dark, nervous eyes. The man saw the floating branch and frowned at it. Lifting his long, slender pole, he pushed the muddy, dripping end of it toward the drifting, half-visible branch.

Riot inhaled soundlessly and went completely underwater, holding the dynamite an inch or two clear of the river. In momentary indecision, he waited for the prying pole to push through the branch and reach the explosives in his dry hand. But the pole did not touch him.

And then he heard two distinct shots somewhere above the water, followed an instant later by a barrage of gunfire.

Easing his head back up, the first thing he saw was the small boat, now within reach. It was moving at a grotesque angle, since one of the boatmen was lying over one side, half in and half out of the water. He was dead. The second was leaning unsteadily on his pole. As Riot breathed in some air, the second man let go of the pole and splashed into the water.

On the raft a short distance beyond the boat, several men were firing toward the shore. Riot heard Bud command angrily, "Stop shootin'! Don't want 'im hittin' this flatboat, God damn it!" He yelled to Vinaro on the other side of the river, "There's jus' one man! He shot them fellows in the boat an' then stopped shootin'!"

Vinaro and Blood Shirt were in the center of a growing mob on the Comanche side. The Mexican turned to one of his men and said furiously, "Ask Blood Shirt if this is a trick to get the guns without paying for them."

The other man spoke rapidly in Comanche to the big Indian in the red shirt. Blood Shirt answered in a low voice that Riot could not hear.

"No!" Vinaro shouted after a quick translation. "I don't want his braves going across the river! Tell him we'll take care of that man ourselves!" He yelled across the Conchos in loud, rapid Spanish, and after a moment there was an answering shout.

Riot and the branch came against the aimlessly floating boat, and a few seconds later it touched the edge of the big raft. Bud said, "Somebody grab that boat," and Riot tugged at the branch so that it drifted free toward the shadowed side of the raft. The barrels were on this side, looming above him in the night. He raised the dynamite and left the branch to float on by itself. Pulling himself partly out of the water, he placed the dynamite deep in the black shadows between two kegs of gunpowder.

"What's that?" Bud's voice demanded.

"What's what?" a thick, tense voice replied.

Riot dropped soundlessly back down, taking a breath as he went unhurriedly back into and under the water. He heard several shots above, but no bullets came near him. Waiting until his breath was gone, he came back up at the side of the raft.

"Jesus! Shootin' at a branch!" Bud grumbled.

"You started it," the tense voice complained. "Askin' stupid questions!"

There were shots from the Mexican side of the river now, and Bud said, "They got sighta who done that shootin'."

Riot raised head and shoulders up over the edge of the raft, moving as fast as he could with no noise. His hands were too wet to touch the fuse, so he rubbed them together, then rubbed them along the sides of the kegs of powder at the raft's edge before him. The shooting at the Mexican edge of the river started again, and he judged Tad was giving them a fight.

Unwinding the long fuse he'd tied to the firecracker's three-inch fuse, it occurred to Riot that the longer fuse would have the smaller chance of success. It might burn out at some point. It might be noticed by one of the men on the raft. But if he lit only the three-inch fuse, it would explode before the men could even get to this side of the raft. He hesitated. He was almost dead anyway. What difference did it make? Cordenas and Ruiz had both looked at him and known that he was not afraid of death. Gritting his teeth together, he arched his head back and looked at the stars twinkling above the dark, rounded rims of powder kegs. Even one more hour of living would be a good thing.

He took one of the matches from the cloth around the dynamite. When he tried to strike it, cupping his hands over it so the light would not show, the tip of the match rubbed off without lighting. Damp. The second match was dry enough to light, and he let the flame of it burn the palm of his left hand rather than have the glare show above the powder kegs. He touched it to the end of the four-foot fuse and then softly blew the match out.

Vinaro yelled, "One of you men get in that boat and bring it over! They may be all night killing that man!"

"Okay," Bud called back.

And then Riot filled his lungs and went back under the water, swimming under the surface and downstream so that the current was at his back.

When his lungs were fiercely hot and tight for want of air, he at last came up, far downstream from the raft. There was now a great deal of shooting behind him, and frantic shouts from both sides of the river and from the raft.

There was a large boulder, about eight feet high, that jutted out a few feet from the bank and into the river. Riot swam as fast as he could for the rock, and he touched ground behind it as a tremendous, ear-bursting, breath-crushing force slammed at him from all sides.

On the Conchos, the raft disappeared in a thunderous, booming blast that sent a vast wall of river water flying in every direction. The Comanche tents more than a thousand feet away were flattened instantly, and Indian ponies far across the wide flat were knocked down by the earthquaking power of the huge explosion, only to get up filled with terror, and race madly into the hills beyond.

At the Mexican side of the river, where animals and wagons had been closer to the edge of the water, almost nothing was left. The wagons had been picked up and thrown as if by a giant hand, splintered, broken and crushed against rocks and trees and the earth itself. The few animals who were not dead or injured staggered to their feet and ran wildly away from the scene of mammoth violence.

A surge of frothing water picked Riot up and carried him a hundred feet before dashing him down on the bank of the river. Before him, the Conchos went crazy. The huge wave sped on downstream, and after it was gone, the river ran backwards. Riot realized numbly it was a backwash, filling in the lower level of water where the explosion had taken place. Something flashed through the moonlight and landed soundlessly a few feet to his side, and Riot realized that part of the reason for the unearthliness of what he saw was that he could hear nothing. He studied the thing at his side and finally stretched out his hand and picked it up. It was a twisted gunbarrel. It was faintly hot to his touch. And then his ears began to ring in a high-pitched scream that seemed to come from the middle of his head.

When the ringing at last stopped, he could hear gunfire and hideous shrieks from upriver at the site of the Comanche camp – or what was left of it. As he listened, the gunfire stopped and there was a sharp, agonized cry that broke suddenly into a loud, terrible gurgle. And then there was only a babble of frightened, excited voices, with no one sound penetrating above the others.

There was the sound of horses' hoofs, and suddenly Tad riding his black appeared in the moonlight along the river. He was leading Riot's pinto. Holding both of the horses' reins, he got down and leaned over Riot. "Were you hurt?"

"My head. But it was never much good anyway." Riot started to get up, and fell back down. "Nothing's broken. I'll be okay in a minute."

"Thought that fellow hit ya, shootin' off the raft there." Tad stood up to stare back at the Indian camp. "Doubt there's a Comanchero left alive. Those as wasn't killed outright by the blowup, got tore to pieces by the Indians."

"Those on this side of the river?"

"I shot the ones that was after me. Never even saw no trace of them that was standin' by the river. Vinaro and Blood Shirt got blown clear to the Gulf of Mexico."

Tad leaned down. "I'll help you mount up. We gotta get out of here."

As the older man leaned forward, Riot felt a drop of warm liquid hit his arm. He sat up and pulled on the boots Tad handed him. His numbed muscles were obeying him now, his head no longer ringing. He stood on his feet and said, "You bleeding?"

"A little. Got hit shallow in the arm. Let's go."

"Better wrap it."

There was a sudden, wild shout from across the Conchos. A Comanche appeared at the river's edge and let fly an arrow that landed before them in the water with a whipping sound.

"No time now!" Tad swung to saddle and Riot leaped aboard the pinto without putting his foot in the stirrup. They rode away from the river as the first Comanche waded out toward them. The bank became alive with other warriors, all on foot.

At a point high on a hill overlooking the Conchos, the two men turned to see what was happening behind them. One of the Comanches, a strong swimmer, had crossed the river with the help of an end of long rope. He'd tied it to a tree and others were swimming hand over hand on it across the water.

"They ain't got no horses just now," Tad said, "but they can run like wolves. We better hightail it."

The two men rode into the dark at a fast lope, afraid to let their horses out full until they came to more even ground. Some time later, Tad called out from behind Riot, "Wait up!"

Riot slowed his paint and brought it to a stop. "What's the matter?"

"That — that bleedin's worse'n —" Tad's face was white in the moonlight. He opened his mouth to continue speaking, then rolled out of the saddle onto the ground.

A quarter of a mile before them lay wide flatlands over which they'd be able to travel at top speed. But there was no place to hide there. Riot looked around him, then picked Tad up with one arm, letting his feet drag, and led the horses with the other hand. He moved into a rough, triangular niche in a steep hillside to his left. There he tied the horses to a stout bush of greasewood and started to tear Tad's sleeve to get a look at his wound. The sleeve was so soaked with blood that it was slippery and hard to rip, but Riot soon exposed the bullet wound. It was high on the left arm, on the inside, and blood was coming from it in lazy spurts. Riot tore the sleeve into strips and tied the first one tight above the wound. The spurting stopped. Then Riot wrapped a wider piece of the cloth around the wound itself and tied it firm.

After a moment, Tad opened his eyes. He stared up through the dark at Riot and said in a voice so weak it was hard to make out his words. "You better get on your way."

"We'll rest just a minute. Let you get your strength back."

"Comanches'll be on top of us in ten minutes." Tad's voice, even in its ghostlike thinness, took on a note of desperation. "I ain't got the power to lift a gun! You won't stand a chance!"

"Can you hang onto your horse if I hoist you up?"

"No."

"Then I'll tie you on."

Riot picked Tad up and heaved him into the saddle on the black. He took the lariat from the saddle and lashed Tad's hands to the horn, then he tied the boots firmly into the stirrups, drawing the rope tight from one foot to the other under the horse's belly.

Tad could see clearly, though he was almost lying over the black's neck, and he said, "They're out there! I just saw a whole line of 'em."

Riot glanced out at the shallow, sloping valley before them that led down to the flats. They were still far away, but the entire slope was covered with shadowy figures. They were moving in a slow, cautious line, one and two deep, toward the niche in the steep hill where Riot and Tad were concealed.

"Those bastards can run, all right," he murmured. He turned his head from side to side. The dirt wall behind him and those to each side were too steep for a horse to climb, but they were not too steep for a man to slide down.

"They're all around us," Tad whispered. "Comin' in in a big circle."

"All we got to do is bust through one part of that circle." Riot took the gunny sack from his own saddle pommel and reached for the thick canvas bag. "Maybe we can scare 'em some. They already had one fright. They oughtta be about set to admit this ain't a night the gods are on their side." He spilled the contents of the canvas bag onto the ground.

Tad couldn't make out any distinct objects in the pile of things that Riot was leaning over, but he heard Riot mutter, "My God! I thought this was just firecrackers!"

"More dynamite?" he asked in a small voice.

"Better, maybe."

Tad stared at the slope. The Comanches were closer now, and as the circle became smaller, the line became thicker. They were now four and five deep as they crept toward the niche.

Riot was on his knees a few feet before the horses, near the opening of the pocket in the steep hill, and he was working frantically. When the closest Comanches were almost within speaking distance, there was the small bright flare of a match in Riot's hand, and then he was running back to the horses.

In the stillness broken only by Riot's running footsteps there came suddenly a ghastly, barking war cry from one of the nearest Comanches, who stood up full height from his crouching advance and waved a shadowy arm toward the slope. The great ring of braves took up the chilling scream and the sound came to Riot and Tad from all directions as the Comanches charged.

Riot snatched the reins from the greasewood brush and leaped onto his pinto, twisting the black's reins around his left hand.

There was a sudden, blinding flash of light that was combined with a terrifying *whoosh* of sound that drowned out the savage war cries.

Like a furious demon, the expanding, shooting light sped angrily straight at the Comanches, leaving a long, burning trail of fire scorching the air behind it.

Another burning devil, this time blue, moved hideously on a burst of sound toward the Comanches. It went sizzling past a brave's head and the brave screamed with sheer terror, threw down his war club and ran shrieking away.

"Come on, horses!" Riot spurred his frightened pinto and sped out of the niche with Tad's black straining rebelliously at the lead reins. Two more rockets went off as he galloped out onto the slope. One of them burst into a great, devilish fist of varicolored lights that descended toward the Comanches with a boom and distinct poppings. Dozens of firecrackers banged, boomed and cracked in a wild crescendo, and a large pinwheel blazed suddenly to life, whizzing into a huge, noisy circle of light that sent red, blue, green and yellow sparks soaring high into the air in all directions.

Out of the bursting, flaming niche, Riot charged like a fiend straight from hell. He threw back his head and roared, "Yeeeeeeoww!" and thundered straight at the Comanches.

Horror-stricken, they scattered before him, dropping their weapons and yowling in complete panic.

Whooping like a devil, Riot ran right over one warrior who was too paralyzed to move. He hit the flat at a full gallop and sped out across the open land. The horses needed no encouragement. They stuck their noses straight out before them, and their tails trailed straight out behind them as they tore away from the dreadful sights and sounds.

Only when the horses were lathered with sweat and in danger of dying from a longer run, did Riot pull them down to a trot, and finally a walk. They rode all night, making the best speed possible. From time to time Riot stopped the horses so that he could lean over and loosen the tourniquet on Tad's arm, but other than that there were no stops in their long ride. . . .

The early-morning sun warmed them as the horses walked, sore and tired, to the north. Riot looked at Tad with concern. "Could you eat some jerky if I untie your hands?"

"Maybe."

The beef helped Tad, and after a while he said, "I was damned near as scared as those Comanches. Didn't know what was goin' on at first."

"We just celebrated the Fiesta of St. Matthew a little early."

Tad rubbed his aching hands and wrists, then took the canteen from his saddle and drank some water. "I feel better. Drink?"

"Yeah."

When Riot handed the canteen back, Tad said, "How you feelin'?"

"Rotten."

"Infection?"

"Yeah. Also, someplace in my goddam big ears, I can still hear that explosion echoing. I should've given it six or seven feet of fuse."

"What?"

"I said I should've given it more fuse. Given myself time to get further away."

"You mean you set the fuse? The way you started out t'do?"

Riot looked at him, puzzled. "Well, what in hell do you think set it off?"

Tad snorted and shrugged his shoulders. "Well, my hunch last night was that they'd shot you, or you'd got the stuff in your hand wet, or somethin'. I waited, fightin' a sort of runnin' fight with them two Mexicans chasin' me, to give you time to get clear if you were still kickin'. Then after I shot them, I was back pretty far, but I started shootin' at the raft. It blew just about the right time after a shot I'd taken that felt pretty good to my eye."

"Then that was you they were all shooting at when I came up from swimmin' underwater."

"Guess so. I never hope to get shot at so

much again." Tad took hold of the pommel as a faint weakness came over him again. "But if you set your dynamite off on the raft, it was you blew the place up."

Riot held the pinto to a very slow walk for a moment so that he could unwrap the black's reins from his left hand and pass them over the horse's head to Tad. "It seemed to me it took a little longer than it should've for the fuse to burn. I got a hunch it went out, and your slug did the trick."

Tad shook his head dubiously. "Actually, that was a hell of a long shot I took."

Riot grinned. "We'll never know."

The Last Month

12

They rode north toward Ojinaga, and each day Tad became stronger, until he was finally as fit as he had ever been. But each day too, Riot became worse. There was no lessening of his strength, nor was there great pain, but the infection in the lower part of his chest sometimes bothered him, and it was constantly becoming more inflamed, more swollen.

In Presidio, Riot said, "Time for a general overhaul. Horses' shoes are so thin they got only one side. An' you and me look like the wrath of God."

They left the animals at the blacksmith shop to be shod, and then got store-bought shaves and haircuts, and bathed in hot water. Riot bought new shirts and jackets for them both. He even bought Tad a black string tie, "So you can make a good show for Roslyn."

"Well then, ain't you gonna get one that'll do the same thing?"

"Nope." Riot said no more.

Looking like new men, they mounted and started out of Presidio. Partway up the block, the two Rangers they'd seen before walked out into the street to stop them.

"Good trip?" the older one asked.

"Fair," Riot said.

"How was Brazil?" The man shifted his gaze to Tad.

Tad shrugged. "Fulla nuts."

The younger Ranger stiffened, and Tad said, "If I have to beat you up again, I'll do a job of it."

Riot leaned over the pommel of his saddle. "Mister, why don't you ask about what you're really interested in? Rifles, isn't it?"

The older man's voice hardened. "You know anything about any rifles?"

"Yeah."

The Ranger rubbed thoughtfully at his jaw. "Reason I didn't ask outright, I can't talk over every border problem with every man who crosses it. Lots of times the best thing to do is talk about the weather, keep a close look on the fellow, and draw your own conclusions about him. What do you know about rifles?"

"I can tell you, you got nothing more to worry about on that score."

"Why not?"

" 'Cause they ain't around any more." Riot started to build a cigarette with some Bull Durham and brown cigarette paper he'd bought. "Neither is Blood Shirt."

"How do you know?"

"That's a long story. And you wouldn't believe it."

"We could throw you in jail," the younger man said, his earlier anger gone.

"No, you couldn't." Riot finished the smoke and put a match to it. "Because I don't feel like going to jail. I ain't got the time." He looked steadily from one to the other. "Way things are, I'd kill you first."

The older man nodded. "I guess you would kill us — or have a good try at it. And it ain't worth it. You're not carrying a stack of rifles under your arm, which is about all we could jail you on for more than a couple of days."

"If you had somethin' to do with it," the younger Ranger said, "why don'cha speak up? Might get your name in the history books."

"Fellows who write the history books wouldn't believe it, either."

They picked up the reins and moved on, leaving the two lawmen in the street. When they were out of Presidio, Tad said, "That didn't sound like you. Bein' kind of nice and gentle with them Rangers."

"Didn't sound like you, either," Riot told him. "Nuts in Brazil." He shook his head. "You're getting to be a real concern to me, with your contrariness, and trying to get in fights and such."

Nearing Alpine, Riot said, "We'll skirt it this time."

"Been a long time between drinks."

"You speaking for me or for you?"

Tad considered the question. "Both, I guess."

"Well I got you this close to home safe and sound. No point getting you hung now."

They went around the town and moved north toward Fort Davis. On the day that they approached the fort, Riot said, "I'll be leaving you here. You can cut over to the settlement. I'm going on north."

"Where?"

"I don't know. North."

"What'll you do?"

"Damned if I know."

"Roslyn and me'll probably be buildin' up the old place, tryin' to make out of it what Ma and Pa wanted to make — a good ranch with good cattle."

"What's that got to do with me?"

"We'd like to have you with us." Tad watched the fort looming slowly closer and pushed back a choking lump in his throat. "You oughtta be with people who love you."

"I told you I'm going to go out with a bang. You can't raise any real hell with people you like hanging around, especially if one's a girl." Riot sighed loudly. "Jesus. I'm goin' to go north and bust up a few places. Do a particular lot of gambling and drinking, which are two things I'm fallin' way behind on. Find me some wild females. Maybe I'll blow up that town of Tooele, where I was born, just for fun. It'd only take a couple of firecrackers."

They got to the fort and Tad said, "Before goin' on over to the settlement, I'm goin' to stop in now and see Colonel Blacker. Tell 'im the rifles're broke up an' lyin' along the bottom of the Conchos."

Riot turned his pinto away from the gate. "Well, I'll see you later."

"Wait a minute!" Tad groped for words. "Wait a minute. Come on in. Soon's I see the colonel, I'll ride north with you a little farther before cuttin' over to the settlement."

Riot said, "Well, okay," and rode into the fort with Tad. He didn't bother getting down at the hitching-post. Starting to roll a smoke, he said,

"I'll wait here for you."

Tad went into the building which housed Colonel Blacker's quarters. He was gone only a short while. He came back out of the building and started to unhitch his black. "Colonel's not at the fort no more. Transferred to Washington. They got some dumb-lookin' bastard in there in 'is place, never been west of the Big Muddy. Can't talk to him."

There was a small group of officers passing by, and one of them left the others to come to the hitching-rail. He was an older man, slender and stern-faced. He put out his hand and said, "Thaddeus McCallister," and then Riot recognized him as the Army surgeon, Dr. Gates.

Tad shook hands with him. "Good to see you, sir." He nodded at Riot, still sitting his paint. "You recall my friend Riot Holiday."

"Indeed I do." The old doctor squinted up into the afternoon sun. "I see you've been following doctor's orders."

Riot shifted uncomfortably in the saddle. At last he said, "Yes."

"How have you been?"

"All right."

Tad said, "He's got a bad infection that's been troublin' him. Why don't you take a look at it?"

"Not worth the bother," Riot muttered.

"By all means."

Tad reached for the reins looped around the pinto's saddlehorn. "I'll tie 'em. Get down. Maybe he can help you."

Riot's face was full of argument, but the reins were now out of his hands, and he stepped down off the paint. "Ain't worth the bother," he repeated to the doctor.

"My office is over here."

Inside the doctor's office, Tad said, "It's low on his chest. Beneath that old arrow wound."

Doctor Gates nodded. "Really? Cut yourself, Mr. Holiday?"

"Just rubbed it on some rock."

"Take off your shirt."

The doctor glanced at the large swelling as Riot finished stripping to the waist. Then the old man frowned, moving closer to get a better look at the inflamed area. "There is an operating table behind you, Mr. Holiday. Will you lie down on it?"

When Riot was stretched out on the table, the doctor touched the swollen place, feeling at it gently. "Hurt?"

"You're damn right."

The doctor was fascinated by the inflammation now. He studied it from every possible angle, often leaning so close to it that his nose almost touched Riot. Finally, the old man said, "Son of a bitch!"

"It serious?" Tad asked him.

Gates ignored the question. "Mr. Holiday, I'm going to do something that is going to hurt." He took a small bottle from a glassed-in shelf behind him and dabbed some colorless liquid over the swollen area. Then he reached for a short-bladed knife in the same cabinet.

"I ain't about to lay here and get cut up," Riot said, his voice irritated.

The doctor pushed his head back onto the table. He said firmly, "Shut up. Lie still." He drew the knife across the center of the red swelling.

"Ow!" Riot yelped, as Gates pushed with both hands toward the center of the area he had lanced. "You better be finished, 'cause I sure as hell am!"

Gates said, "Shut up!" He stared at his right hand and said in an awe-stricken voice, "God almighty!"

"What is it?" Tad demanded.

Riot was up now on his elbows. He glanced at the narrow slit the doctor had cut. A thin line of blood was coming from it. "You going to stand there an' stare at your hand all day, while I bleed to death?" he asked.

Gates looked at him finally, his eyes blank with wonderment. He held out his hand for Riot to see.

Cupped in the hand, within a thin film of transparent covering, was a steel arrowhead.

There was dead silence in the room for several minutes. Dr. Gates wordlessly handed the arrowhead to Riot, who stared at it dumbly. Tad came to Riot's side. His lips parted slightly and he put his hand on Riot's shoulder.

Dr. Gates automatically put a small bandage on the incision he'd made, then nodded at Riot, who got up and put his shirt back on.

It was Riot who at last broke the silence. "Guess I'll keep it as a good luck piece," he said, dropping the pointed piece of steel in his pocket.

Dr. Gates almost exploded with the question, "What in hell have you been doing since I saw you last?"

"He's been gettin' himself knocked all over the place," Tad said. "He's been hit an' butted an' bombed an' kicked an' slugged. And he's done a hundred times more back to them as what was doin' it to him. He's been in the saddle damn near straight through except when he's been fightin' or making love or working with a sledge hammer or getting drunk or knocking a hole through a stone wall practically with his bare fists." Tad paused. "That," he concluded, "is how he's been livin' up to doctor's orders."

"I can't believe it," Gates murmured. "It's incredible. When I first examined you, such a simple thing as falling down should have killed you."

"Riot's as tough as leather," Tad said.

The doctor shook his head. "There's more to it than that. It's a common thing for the body to eject foreign matter. In the war I saw many men who had small bits of shrapnel in them, usually flesh wounds, and the metal was forced out of the body from within. But an object as deep as that – lodged next to the heart! And an object as big as that!"

"Well," Tad repeated, "I tell you, he's a rugged fellow."

"No. There's more." Gates looked, still unbelieving, at the hand that had held the arrowhead. "There's a special chemistry in some men, a fierce will to live. And it's damned near impossible to kill those men. They, and their bodies, cling to life and push death away, when other men would be long gone." He took a deep breath and let it out slowly. "There's no understanding it. All you can do is recognize it – and wonder about it."

Riot and Tad left Dr. Gates a little later. They went to the hitching-rail and untied their horses and swung up to saddle.

They rode out of the fort, and Tad swung his horse gently to the east, glancing at Riot to see if he would complain about heading toward the settlement. Riot swung alongside of him without a word, and Tad smiled briefly and they moved along to where the land became more and more familiar.

The fort was out of sight behind them when Riot spoke for the first time since he'd said the arrowhead would be a good luck piece. He kept his eye on the path before them and said, "Being as you're Roslyn's brother, it's only fair for you to know ahead of time. I'll go on to the settlement with you, under the circumstances, and I'll stay around a while. I might even help you and her get the ranch back in shape. And if Roslyn and me get to going around together a little, and maybe things get serious with us, why, I'll reform. But what I want you to know as her brother, and ahead of time, is that I'll never reform a hell of a lot." Riot took the arrowhead from his pocket. It was still slightly damp, and he rubbed it on his shirt to dry it. He tossed it in the air and caught it and put it back in his pocket. Then he grinned. "You know," he said, "life is a fine thing."